MORE ABOUT THOSE CRAZY KIDS
Who Are *Courting Trouble*
on the *Road to Romance*
by raising *Mayhem and Magic*

Angelica Cruthers — *sharp, witty, with candy-box looks that belie her keen intelligence*

May De Vere — *shy and quiet, May develops confidence when the others respect her insight and wisdom*

Peter De Vere — *May's elder brother, handsome, reserved, with a hidden depth of feeling, especially for Angelica*

Hallie Meadows — *a city girl, sophisticated in manner but with a heart as big as all outdoors*

Jess O'Brien — *talented, creative, introspective, totally unaware of his own charisma*

Eustice Smith — *a born busybody with more brains than common sense. His energy and enthusiasm challenge and vitalize the others, definitely a catalyst*

Rachel Smith — *Eustice's cousin, intelligent, balanced, practical*

Don't miss the antics of these super sleuths in the coming Hart Mysteries.

Dear Readers:

Thank you for your unflagging interest in First Love From Silhouette. Your many helpful letters have shown us that you have appreciated growing and stretching with us, and that you demand more from your reading than happy endings and conventional love stories. In the months to come we will make sure that our stories go on providing the variety you have come to expect from us. We think you will enjoy our unusual plot twists and unpredictable characters who will surprise and delight you without straying too far from the concerns that are very much part of all our daily lives.

We hope you will continue to share with us your ideas about how to keep our books your very First Loves. We depend on you to keep us on our toes!

Nancy Jackson
Senior Editor
FIRST LOVE FROM SILHOUETTE

A Hart Mystery

RACHEL'S RESISTANCE
Nicole Hart

Published by Silhouette Books New York
America's Publisher of Contemporary Romance

First Love from Silhouette

For Nancy-Dabney Jackson
Editor Supreme

SILHOUETTE BOOKS
300 E. 42nd St., New York, N.Y. 10017

ISBN: 0-373-06209-5

First Silhouette Books printing November 1986

America's Publisher of Contemporary Romance

Printed in the U.S.A.

RL 4.4, IL age 10 and up

Visit France in
Rachel's Resistance
Book #4 of
The Hart Mysteries
by
Nicole Hart

NICOLE HART was born in Georgia. As a child, she lived in both Northern and Southern states before making New York her home. Blessed with an insatiable curiosity, Ms. Hart is an ardent traveler. She has wandered all over the United States, Canada and Europe. The various exotic settings of her Hart Mysteries have been enjoyably researched, as you can see by the authentic maps in each Hart Mystery. Her six lively characters are based on old, dear friends. We think that you, too, will take them to your heart.

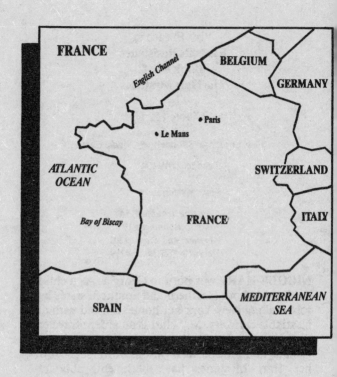

Chapter One

"Where is Eustice hiding now?"

Rachel Smith turned to Angelica Cruthers. A frustrated look marred the gentle lines of her face. "He was right here a minute ago."

"I bet."

"But he *was*, Angelica. And he said that he wouldn't move an inch until I came back with the gas for our mopeds."

"Solexes. Remember we're in France now and we must not fall into Americanisms. The French call them Solexes. Remember, we promised our parents not to speak one word of English the whole summer."

"Yet we speak English most of the time."

"Not at breakfast, we don't. The viscount was sharp with me for even saying the word 'honey' in English."

"So you didn't speak again for the entire meal, Angelica. You call that speaking French?"

"I call that *not* speaking English." Both of them laughed.

"Well, we have only just arrived. They can't expect us to blast right into fluent *français*."

"Oh yes they can. My parents told them to show me no mercy." Angelica sighed. "I guess they were tired of seeing my report card ruined by low grades in French, but I've never been able to master languages. I think you either have the ability or you don't."

"That's the most ridiculous thing I've ever heard you say— Eustice! Where have you been?"

Eustice Smith had come up behind them and was standing there holding two long French baguettes and some packages wrapped in white paper.

"I thought you weren't going to move an inch!" Rachel remonstrated.

"Even to pack a picnic lunch?" Eustice waved one of the loaves. "Madame la Vicomtesse called to me from the second floor to say that she had ordered two extra loaves of bread for us to take with us today. When I went into the kitchen to get them I saw that Danielle had also left us some cheese and sausage."

"So that's what she was saying," Angelica said under her breath.

"You mean you knew where he went?" Rachel turned to her, surprised.

"No, I didn't know where he went. I know that Madame d'Ambert leaned out from her bedroom and spoke very rapidly in French and that Eustice disappeared. Then you came back with the gas and asked me where he was hiding out—"

"I can see that you are going to be of no use to us as a translator, Angelica."

"Why give out false information to save my pride? I know I can't speak French. You know I can't speak French. We've been in France for four days and suddenly everyone expects me to speak fluently."

"You could have said that he was going to the kitchen to get some food."

"But I didn't know that, Rachel! All I knew was that he took off like a missile and disappeared around the corner of the château before I could even remember *Où vas-tu?*—or whatever you say when you want to know where the heck someone is going."

"That's right, Angelica. That's just what you say when you want to know where the heck I'm going." Eustice grinned at her.

"Can we go now?" Angelica eyed the Solexes. "These look like fun. I've always wanted to ride one, only my mother would never let me."

"She can't say anything to you now, *chérie*. These are our only means of transportation and your mother is out of reach at the moment." Rachel went over and got on her Solex. "How do you start these up?"

"You flick the switch on and then pedal while moving the handle that controls gas and speed." Eustice demonstrated by getting on his bike, and slowly pedaling until the bike's motor caught and started with a smoky, spluttering buzz. The girls pedaled rapidly after him. Within seconds their Solexes had purred into life and the three rode down the long driveway away from the crumbling old château.

Riding under the towering trees that lined the driveway all the way to the rickety old gate, Rachel felt a wave of excitement. This was her first time in Europe and already France was matching her dreams of how it would be. Just as old, just as beautiful, just as French—she sighed happily and accelerated to catch up with the other two.

Eustice had pulled up to a stop at the gateway, his Solex buzzing smoothly. Rachel could see that through his thick glasses his eyes were shining.

"Which direction should it be?" he asked.

"Right!"

"Left!"

Eustice laughed. "Do you think you girls could agree on this?"

Angelica grinned at Rachel. "Shall we let him choose?"

Rachel nodded. "Either way is fine with me."

Eustice gunned his motor and turned to the left. "Tally ho!"

"Say that in French, *s'il vous plaît*!" Rachel reminded him.

"Tall*ez*-ho!"

"See? You're already sounding authentic!"

"*Mais oui*, but yes," Eustice shouted above the motor's buzz. "Already I'm in love with this country!"

"You've gone only ten feet into it."

"But look, Rach, how beautiful it is."

The small country road that they had turned onto passed through summer fields alive with wildflowers. The local farms made patterns throughout the gentle hills. Here and there rich soil had been plowed open and the smell of warm grass and manure overwhelmed their senses. Smelling, Rachel decided, was as exciting in France as seeing and tasting.

"Cows ahead!" Eustice cried, slowing down his Solex.

A farmer was moving his herd across the road from one field to another. The sound of bells and gentle mooing attended the clip-clop of their hooves on the road.

"*Bonjour!*" Eustice waved.

The old man said something in response that was lost in the sounds of the cows and the bikes. As they passed the spot where the herd was going through the gate into the new field, Eustice waved one of the loaves over his head like a sword. *"Vive la France!"* he called.

"I don't understand one word he's saying," Angelica grumbled.

"But you understand his face and his expression, don't you? That's the first step to fluency."

"Then I have a long way ahead of me." Angelica laughed.

Rachel pulled up next to her, keeping her bike moving at the same speed. "We have the whole summer, Angelica. When we go home no one will recognize us."

"That is, if they are blindfolded and we alter our voices."

"It is just that attitude that made you flunk French in the first place," Eustice said.

"I wish Peter were here instead of you," she retorted.

"It's good for you to be without him! You two have been seeing each other for too long."

"Wait till you fall for a girl, Eustice."

"Never! I'd never let a girl make a monkey out of me."

"Too late to worry about that, Eustice!" Rachel laughed.

"Well, I only hope it happens this summer," Angelica said. Oblivious of Angelica's scrutiny, Eustice was riding about twenty feet ahead. He still wore his thick glasses, but Angelica noticed that he had changed over the past year. The winter had added inches to his frame, making him tall and overly thin. His hair was its usual wild curling light brown, but it seemed to suit him better now. Perhaps it was because the fingers that constantly ran through it had grown into the sensitive long hands of a man.

"You know, Rachel, in a few years your cousin is going to be pretty good-looking."

"Good. Then maybe he'll be kinder about what he now refers to as 'that boy-girl garbage.'"

"And won't we get even?"

"You bet!" They smiled at each other.

The three young people explored their new environment all morning, riding through the small town of Trange that lay within eight kilometers of Le Mans. Refilling the Solexes' small tanks they began to search for the perfect spot for a picnic. The sun was high overhead when Eustice pointed to an empty field. They turned their bikes off the road and followed him to a large tree in its center. They leaned their bikes against it while Eustice pulled out the French bread and opened the white wrapped packages that held cheese and sausage. They had stopped at a local market and bought fresh tomatoes, fruit and soft drinks, which he now placed decoratively on an old cotton tablecloth bedspread beside the swift-running stream. Angelica pulled out her camera and snapped a photograph of the two cousins smiling happily as they reclined under the shade of the tree.

When they had finished lunch, they all rested for an hour or two, Eustice scribbling feverishly in his journal while Angelica wrote home. Rachel just lay on her back looking up through the leaves of the tree to the bright blue French sky until she fell asleep. She awoke suddenly as a cloud passed over the late afternoon sun.

"We'd better head back," Eustice said, as Rachel's eyelids began to flutter sleepily again.

It was early evening by the time they reached the gateway of the château.

"Can you imagine what this place was like two centuries ago?" Eustice asked, admiring the turreted silhouette against the evening sky.

"Can you imagine living in a house that existed two centuries ago?" Rachel asked.

"You're sounding very American."

"I *am* American."

"Not for the summer, you're not. You're French. That's the deal we made with our families to get them to send us here."

"That and the fact that you're related to the viscount, Eustice."

"Not related, actually. His sister lived with Rachel's and my grandparents' family during the war."

"Was she nice?" Rachel asked. "The viscount seems so stiff."

"Didn't your father know her too?" Angelica asked.

"Not really. My father was in the navy; Eustice's father was the baby and stayed home during most of the war. He was the one who knew Simone."

"I never met her," Eustice continued. "She stayed until Paris was liberated and then returned. But she and my father always wrote each other at Christmas. She died a couple of years ago as I remember."

"How did your family know that the viscount and viscountess were taking in summer guests?" Rachel asked. "I thought it was through her."

"No, the viscount wrote my dad to tell him that Simone had died and in the letter he mentioned that they were taking in students for the summer to help with expenses."

"Do you think we'll be the only ones this summer?"

Eustice nodded. "I think so. Last night at dinner the viscount mentioned something about his son who is due to arrive soon. I also think he mentioned another château in the area that took in other students."

"You understood all that?"

"Angelica, didn't you get any of what he was saying?"

"I got the part about the other château and a bit about the son. Only I couldn't understand whether he just had a son or whether the son was actually going to be around."

They pulled up to the house and parked their Solexes near the back kitchen door. "What next?" Rachel asked, looking at her watch. "We have a while before dinner."

"Why don't we explore a bit?" Eustice suggested. "We really haven't had time to look around."

"Inside or outside?"

"Outside. We can always explore the inside on a rainy day."

"It's hard to tell where the château stops and the farm begins," Rachel said.

"That's because the château is both."

"But I thought châteaus were supposed to be large and more—sophisticated," Angelica said.

"You're thinking of the castles in the Loire Valley. I think that there are many châteaus that are the manor houses of a large farm. I would surmise that the d'Amberts are from a middle level nobility."

"Stop sounding like a guidebook, Eustice," Angelica said crossly. "Anyhow what does middle level nobility really mean?"

"It means that probably one of their ancestors helped the king of France in battle. They got their title and the lands as a reward."

In spite of herself, Angelica was intrigued. "Do you think we could find out?"

"As soon as you learn enough French to ask the viscount."

"That'll take me the entire summer," Angelica said.

"Rachel will translate, won't you, Rach?"

"I got a C-plus in French last year, remember Eustice?"

Eustice stopped. "I forgot. But if I give you all the answers to all the interesting questions, Angelica, you won't have the motivation to ask yourself. Your curiosity is one of your best features. And it's the trait that's going to make you fluent in French by the end of the summer. Mark my words."

"Which means that all I'm going to understand for the first few weeks are Eustice's lectures." Angelica looked over at Rachel. "You're my only hope."

"Unless the son speaks English."

They had been walking down the back driveway, passing the garden, now long overgrown. In the distance they could see the old barn and stable area and next to them was a long low building that appeared to be an enormous garage.

"The carriage house," Eustice said.

"Let's see if there are any left inside," Rachel suggested.

"The doors all look locked from here."

"But there's a broken padlock." Eustice went to the door at the end of the row and pulled it open. It caught on the ground, barely leaving an opening for them to slide through.

"Can you see anything, Eustice?"

"Not yet, my eyes have to adjust." Eustice disappeared inside and almost immediately reemerged. "Come look, there's all kinds of stuff in here!"

They pulled the door as hard as they could, forcing the opening a bit wider for the light. When they knew they couldn't budge it another inch they all slipped into the cool, dusty interior of the old carriage house.

They could see the outline of an old farm wagon. It was missing a wheel and looked as if it had been rotting for years. The back was piled with old rope and with what appeared to be decayed leather harnesses and other battered gear.

"I'd guess that we have about four centuries' worth of clutter in here," Eustice said. "I bet we'd find some pretty cool stuff if we really looked carefully."

"What a nice summer project for you, Eustice," Angelica said.

"Don't be so sarcastic. Hey, what's that?"

"What's what?"

Eustice pointed toward the wagon. "*That.* On the wall over there. It looks like writing or painting of some kind. It's like one huge mural on the wall! I wonder what it could mean?"

Rachel went over to stand next to him. "You're right, Eustice, it's all over the walls and everything. The paintings are quite nice, too."

"We need more light. These figures were painted many years ago."

"And the words, Eustice? Can you read them?" Angelica asked.

Eustice pushed his glasses farther up on his nose and went over to peer more closely at the wall painting. "It isn't French." He paused. "I think it's *German.*"

"There haven't been Germans around here since the war."

"Good thinking, Rachel. I bet that's when that was made. The Germans probably occupied this place."

"Let's ask!" Angelica said.

"What in the world are you children doing in there?" It was the viscountess. Her anxious face peered into the dark. "It's not safe! Come out at once!"

The three scurried guiltily out to find the viscountess standing by the half-open door. In spite of her obvious concern, her face retained its classical beauty. Her brown hair, caught casually in a French twist, accented her high cheekbones and deep brown eyes. Her simple skirt and light shirt open at her slender throat, gave her an almost girlish demeanor.

"*Mes enfants*, you must not go in there, it is not safe—"

"We were just exploring—" Angelica began.

"*En français, chérie!* You must speak to me in French!"

"You tell her, Eustice."

Eustice spoke slowly in French but the viscountess shook her head vehemently.

"What is she saying?" Angelica whispered to Rachel.

"I think she's saying that the carriage house is off-limits."

The viscountess turned to go back to the house. With a fleeting smile she once again shook her head and pointed to the carriage house.

"You must be very careful, the roof will fall any time," she said in English. "I would never be forgiven, you understand?"

"Yes," Angelica said.

"But what does all that German lettering in there mean?" Eustice asked.

"They used this château during the war, *mes enfants*. This was the headquarters for the German army. That was the dining room."

"Holy cow," Eustice whispered.

The viscountess laughed. "You American children are a long way from the war as we saw it. I understand your curiosity, but you must not go in there." She continued seriously, "Your parents want you back home at the end of the summer with no broken bones *s'il vous plaît*."

"Yes ma'am." Angelica gave Eustice a quick glance, and seeing that he was going to say something further, she jabbed him quickly in the ribs.

"Ouch! Angelica, I—"

"We'll be fine, Madame, don't worry about us for a minute," Rachel said firmly.

"*Très bien.* I will leave you now. Enjoy yourselves, my children."

The three watched the viscountess head back toward the house. They waited until she had disappeared before turning to Eustice.

"What were you planning to do, try to talk her into letting us go in there? You know she never will," Rachel said.

"Really, Eustice, I thought you had more sense," Angelica agreed.

Eustice pushed his glasses slowly back up his nose while a grin spread over his face. "You girls are as conniving as I am."

"Of course," Rachel said. "More so. You were about to try to talk her into letting us risk our lives. Which would have made her write our parents and cause a fuss and ultimately ruin the fun."

"Whereas, having said so little, we can soon forget all about it," Angelica added. "And snoop all around as much as we want!"

Eustice shook his head. "And I thought I was the brains in this bunch."

"You are, Eustice, you are," Rachel assured him. "You just have to put the viscountess off our trail." She linked her arm with his and the young people moved slowly toward the front of the house.

Suddenly Eustice pulled Rachel back. "Hey! Isn't that a car I hear?"

Sure enough, down the long driveway came an old dusty Citröen. When it reached the circular section that ran in front of the house it pulled to a stop and the viscount emerged. He was a tall man in his early seventies with a cold expression very unlike his wife's. He spoke sharply to the person getting out of the other side and Rachel could see that it was a young man almost as tall as the viscount.

"Could this be the son?" Angelica whispered.

"Looks like it," Eustice said.

"Not bad," Angelica said.

Rachel could see that the son had his mother's dark coloring and high cheekbones but the aquiline nose was identical to the viscount's. He had just dragged a backpack out of the car when the viscountess came running from the steps to catch him in her arms. Laughing, he lifted her off her feet and swung her around.

"Good-looking *and* nice," Angelica sighed. "Rachel, this one's for you."

"Shush! He's looking this way!" Rachel said.

The viscountess had hooked her arm through her son's and together they were walking toward the front door. He glanced aside. Rachel met his gaze. Had he seen her? She couldn't be sure.

"Wow! If I don't get a letter from Peter this week you're going to have competition!" Angelica whispered.

"Stop it! I don't think he even saw me."

"Well, we'll know a lot more at dinner."

"Meanwhile, if it's all the same to you guys, can we continue our walk?"

"Just lead the way, Eustice, we'll be right behind you."

"By no more than a day or two." Angelica laughed. "Rachel's growing roots staring at sonny."

"If I were you, I'd be a little more discreet," Eustice said.

"What are you talking about? Rachel can stare at anyone she wants."

"Yes, but you'd better note the look on Papa's face."

The viscount was looking at them sharply, refusing to return Eustice's wave.

"I don't think our host is too fond of Americans."

"He hasn't seen our charm yet. Rachel and I will entrance him with our witty conversation."

"You'd better learn to speak French first," Eustice said dryly.

Chapter Two

When Rachel walked into the large dining room that evening she saw the viscount's son was already seated. *"Bonsoir,"* he said, smiling at her.

The viscountess drifted in looking lovely in a soft silk dress with matching sling-back sandals. She slipped behind her son and gave him a quick kiss on the top of his head. Catching Rachel's smile, she returned it. "This is my son, Jean. He is back after a year at school so you must forgive me, yes? We have not seen him since Christmas."

"That's true," Jean said.

"En français, Jean! We promised their parents we would speak only French!"

"But do you understand French?" Jean spoke slowly so that Rachel could understand.

"Yes, a little."

"Then you must tell me your name."

"Je m'appelle Rachel Smith."

"Rachel, a musical name."

Angelica slipped quietly into the seat next to Rachel's. "What did I tell you," she whispered.

"What?" Jean asked.

"Nothing," Rachel said quickly. "This is Angelica Cruthers."

"Hi." Angelica smiled.

"That's *bonsoir* to you, Angelica."

"And that's Eustice Smith," Angelica said, frowning as Eustice took his seat across the table from her.

"You are all related?" Jean asked.

"Not me," Angelica said quickly.

"Gee, Angelica, would you be insulted if I said we were friends?"

Jean laughed. "It isn't necessary, I can tell that by the way you tease one another."

Rachel smiled. "Eustice and I are cousins."

"And your family gave my aunt a home during the war."

"That's right."

The viscount appeared at the door. "Jean, you must not speak English with our guests. It is forbidden."

Rachel met Jean's smile and lowered her eyes. The viscount came in slowly, leaning heavily on his cane, and took his seat at the head of the table. Danielle, a thin, sweet-looking young woman began to serve their dinner. The viscount spoke rapidly with his wife and son. Several times Jean looked angrily at his father. Rachel could tell that there was a great deal of tension between them but always the viscountess's soft voice would intervene, and, with a quick annoyed glance at the three Americans, the viscount would cease his conversation and bite angrily into his food.

After dessert of fresh yogurt and fruit, Eustice rose and in French asked that the three of them be allowed to leave the table. The viscount nodded shortly. Rachel was conscious of Jean's gaze on her back as they walked out.

"Did you understand anything that they said?" Eustice had waited to speak until they were climbing the stairs into the servants' area of the house where their rooms were.

"Not much. The viscount came across as a real bear." Angelica's eyes danced. "And Rachel seems to have captured the fancy of the cub."

"There you go again!" Rachel said. "But seriously, Eustice, did you understand what the viscount and his son were arguing about?"

"Some of it. The old man was lighting into Jean about his studies. I got the sense that the father doesn't approve of his son's interest in art." Eustice stood at the door of his room. "Your room or mine?"

"Ours. There's more space." Rachel led the way a bit farther down the hall where she and Angelica shared an enormous room. The three stepped in. Rachel moved over to the bow windows that looked over the farm.

Aimlessly, she watched the cows being herded back to the smaller paddocks after their evening milking. Her eyes passed over the outlines of the old barn and carriage house.

To her surprise she noticed a figure slipping out of the doorway they had discovered earlier in the day. It was the viscountess! Rachel watched as she fastened a large padlock on the door.

"Good heavens!" she exclaimed.

Eustice flew to her side. "Holy cow! What do you think she's up to?" he asked, clutching Rachel's shoulder.

"That's *sacré vache*, for your information. Please try to keep our promise to our parents! And to answer your question, I haven't a clue."

Angelica joined them at the window but the viscountess had already disappeared from sight.

"*Excusez-moi*, but did I hear you speak English against my father's orders?" Jean was standing there leaning against the door frame, smiling mischievously.

"You sure did," Eustice said.

Jean came in and sat down in one of the old slip-covered easy chairs.

"I like to speak English," he said.

"And you won't tell that we speak it in here?" Angelica asked.

"Of course not. As long as you don't tell them that I speak it in here with you."

"It's a deal," Eustice agreed quickly. "Now, tell us, what's the secret about the carriage house?"

Jean appeared not to have heard the question.

"You're Eustice, yes? An odd name these days, is it not?"

"A horrible name," Eustice said bitterly.

"Have you no other you could use instead?"

"Well, I have a middle name but it's almost as bad."

"Which is?"

"I don't believe it!" Angelica said.

"What?"

"That you're about to get Eustice to tell us his middle name. He's never revealed it to us."

"Byron," Eustice said softly.

"Byron!" Angelica shrieked. "That's even better than I had expected!"

"Shut up, Angelica."

"Eustice Byron Smith? I love it!"

"Angelica—"

"Okay, I'll be good." Angelica giggled. "Byron!"

"My mother was a fan of the Romantic poets. She liked the name Byron and evidently when I was born I had a melancholy expression."

"You still have it. I see it now," Rachel said.

"Angelica could bring it out of anyone."

Angelica ignored him. "Just think, if I call you Byron and then I go away I'd say bye-bye By!"

"I'm going to shoot myself."

"No, you mustn't," Jean said, laughing. "We must talk of other things. And yet I will call you Byron, for I like it."

"I never should have opened my mouth."

"I like it too, Eustice," Angelica chimed in. "It kind of suits your new tall, lean, romantic look."

"My what?"

"Just as soon as you get contact lenses you'll be a knockout."

"I'll never be able to wear them. I'm too blind."

"You still look like a Byron to me."

"No kidding?"

"Not for the world."

Jean laughed. "I like the way you all talk with one another. Is this the American style?"

"You could call it that," Eustice said.

"Could we now discuss the carriage house?" Rachel asked. "Your mother acted so strangely about it today, and just now we saw her padlocking the door."

"I can't imagine why." Jean looked thoughtful. "But I do remember she never allowed me to play in it as a child."

"And all that painting?" Eustice asked. "Was that from the war?"

"Yes indeed. The Germans painted it so that it would look like a real German dining hall."

"Including real Nazi propaganda?" Rachel asked.

Jean's brown eyes caught hers. "That's right."

"I've never been so close to the war before," Eustice said eagerly. "Won't you help us explore?"

"But if they've locked the door—" Jean shrugged.

"We can figure out how to open it!"

"That's our Eustice," Angelica said. "The only breaking and entering expert I know."

"Angelica, it's hardly breaking and entering if Jean goes with us. This is his house."

"How do you always find a way to make lawless behavior seem like the most correct thing in the world?" Angelica asked him.

Jean laughed. "By discussing it with the owner of the house, of course," he interjected. His expression darkened for a moment. "Or his son, that is."

"Your father seems rather set in his ways," Rachel said carefully.

Jean rose to his feet. "Yes. But I must be going."

"Will we see you tomorrow?" Eustice asked.

"I suspect you will see much of me this summer. I want to take you to our neighboring château. They have kids our age and several summer guests like yourselves."

"Are you our age?" Rachel asked him.

"I am sixteen, almost seventeen." He looked down at her. "Is that close enough?"

"That's just right," Eustice said cheerfully.

"Eustice, you're only fifteen."

"Thank you, Angelica, for reminding me."

Jean laughed. "Close enough for me, Byron."

"*À demain*, Jean."

"Yes, till tomorrow."

After Jean had left, Eustice plopped himself down on one of the beds. "I like that guy," he said.

"So do I," Rachel agreed.

"He likes you, too, Rachel, I could tell," Angelica said slyly.

Rachel threw a slipper at Angelica. "You really are the worst troublemaker, Angelica Cruthers."

"Well, you're so pretty Rachel, why wouldn't he?"

Eustice gazed at his cousin seriously. "She's right, Rach."

With a laugh Angelica got up and stretched. "You guys just reminded me I need my beauty sleep. I think I'll go to bed."

"Not a bad idea," Eustice said. "*À demain*, folks."

* * *

Breakfast at the château consisted of toasted day-old French bread with farm-fresh butter and honey. Danielle always left large pots of tea, cocoa and coffee before she went out to do the marketing. A bowl of fresh fruit sat at the center of the table. When they finished, the young people had been instructed to leave their plates on the sideboard for Danielle to wash later.

"I always have wanted to lead this kind of life," Eustice said.

"What, lord of the manor? You're certainly eating like one," Angelica chided.

"I'm a growing man."

"Ten pieces of French bread is a growing man indeed."

"They're small pieces."

"Next to your mouth."

"Angelica, did you wake up on the wrong side of the bed?"

Jean came in looking sleepy.

Eustice grinned. *"Ah, bonjour, Jean!"*

Jean smiled as he went over to the sideboard. "Where is Rachel?"

"Running a little behind schedule." Rachel slipped into her seat.

"Café, mademoiselle?"

"Oui, s'il vous plaît."

"Bonjour, mes enfants. I am glad to be hearing *français* this morning." The viscountess looked

lovely in her morning gown of loose blue and green silk that floated against her body as she went to pour herself a cup of coffee with hot milk. She patted Eustice as she went by him and Rachel could see him swallow quickly and color rise in his cheeks. She desperately wanted to tease him but knew he was too sensitive to endure it in the presence of Madame. She quickly looked over at Angelica to see whether her friend had noticed Eustice's crush and was relieved to see Angelica focusing on her toast and honey. At times Rachel felt surprisingly protective toward her cousin. She knew that his dry wit and intellectual arrogance were only a smoke screen for a loving and tender nature.

"And what are you children going to do today?" the viscountess asked with a smile.

"Continue to explore on our Solexes," Eustice said with an eager look at Jean. "Don't you think?"

Jean nodded. "I also think I might take them over to the Château Menat to see whether the other summer guests have arrived."

"They have," Madame said. "The countess telephoned me yesterday. She says they have prepared the tennis court and that already they are playing all the time."

"Tennis?" Eustice asked weakly.

"But yes, *mon chèr*. Do you like the sport?"

"No."

Madame laughed. "I too have never been much of a player. But the Château Menat has four summer guests so perhaps you will not be forced to play very often."

"I doubt that I will be forced to play at all," Eustice said. "Once people really realize how terrible I am, they rarely ask me to play again."

"You're not that bad, Byron," Angelica said. "You've got a great swing and an impressive backhand. As soon as you actually coordinate that with the ball, you'll be great."

"We call him Bjorn Boring," Rachel said with a giggle.

"Rachel, I never expected it of you. Bjorn Borg was the Lion of Tennis, my father's hero for years. I'm speechless."

"Byron, you're never speechless."

"Quit calling me that."

"*Mes enfants!* Please! You are terrible not to speak French."

"Back to silence," Angelica said.

"*Bonjour*, Papa." Jean stood up as his father came in and slowly made his way to the table. "I will see the rest of you later, yes? We shall meet in half an hour in front of the shed." He turned back to his father.

"Wouldn't it be smarter to leave our Solexes in the carriage house? There is much more room there and we could leave the gasoline containers there too."

"The carriage house is not safe. You are not to go in there." The viscount looked at him coldly. "I will not hear of it."

"My dear, they didn't know," the viscountess said gently. "It is not necessary to be so severe."

"I will not have these children in the carriage house. You must see to it that they understand."

"Papa, our guests will think us rude."

"Jean, you may leave the table."

"I have already left it," Jean said hotly. Turning and catching Rachel's eye, his angry eyes softened for a moment. "I will see you in half an hour?"

"Of course."

Angelica rose. "As a matter of fact—"

"En français!" Eustice commanded.

"You tell them Eustice. I'm going back to my *chambre*."

The viscount spoke rapidly in French and the viscountess waved the children from the room. "Have a nice day," she whispered to Eustice before turning to her husband with a gentle smile. "Roland, your leg is painful today, is it not?"

Rachel heard him respond in softer tones as she left the dining room to catch up with the others.

"Do you think the viscount is hiding something or do you think that he's just the grouchiest man alive?" Eustice asked.

"I think a little bit of both," Rachel said.

"I think he's the grouchiest man alive," Angelica declared.

"Just think of his response to Jean's request."

"Pretty incredible," Rachel agreed. "Let's ask Jean if he knows any more about what happened here during the war. It would be interesting anyway. I could write my summer theme for school about it."

"We could do a project together," Eustice said. "Or use that as an excuse to ask questions."

"All we have to do is bypass the viscount." Angelica shrugged. "Which will be hard."

"And Madame. Remember, she is the one who padlocked the door last night."

"Good point, Rachel. So all we really have is Jean."

"Perhaps Danielle might know something," Eustice said with a gleam in his eye.

"Danielle doesn't speak any English at all," Angelica reminded him.

"Angelica, you really have too little faith. I will write down what I can and the rest I will just sort out somehow. After all, I do have a brain. I may as well practice using it. As you well know, I have been of major help in the solving of three, count them, three mysteries. Rachel will vouch for my unswerving perspicacity in Martha's Vineyard last summer, and if Peter has any mind left at all after dating you for a year, you may ask him to recapitulate on my outstanding performance in Italy two summers ago."

"I was with you, Eustice."

"Then tell Rachel about it. You girls have to have faith in me. I am not the kind of man to be put aside by a language barrier."

"Not when you smell mystery."

Rachel looked from Angelica to Eustice. "What mystery?"

Eustice sat down on the edge of her bed. "Listen, Rach, the way I see it is this. Here we are in France, staying in an old château, the Nazi headquarters during the French occupation of the Second World War. We have proof in the form of an old decaying dining hall that our host and hostess will not let us near. We are dealing with history, and yet our hosts persistently keep trying to get us off the track."

"Off the track of *what*?"

"That's what I aim to find out!"

"Just don't say anything, Rach, let the boy have his fun."

"But Eustice, if we persist in snooping around the carriage house and we don't turn up anything, don't you think we are risking a lot of hassle?"

"If we don't find anything, Rachel, why would the viscount or viscountess be angry with us?" Eustice asked.

"They won't. Unless the roof caves in."

"Which is hardly likely to happen, Angelica."

"Of course, Byron. Why should it? They only *say* it will. Which is, of course, no reason to believe them."

"Angelica, you sang the same tune in Italy."

"And we all know what happened there."

Eustice grinned. "We did have fun, though, didn't we?"

Rachel looked at her watch. "We told Jean we'd meet him now."

"Then let's blast off."

"You forgot your tennis racket," Angelica wickedly reminded Eustice.

"Dear me. I must have buried it somewhere."

"That's okay. I brought two."

Eustice came to a halt. "You didn't!"

Angelica grinned at Rachel.

Rachel laughed. "I get tired just listening to you two. Can we just go quietly downstairs, meet Jean and get on our Solexes to explore? This conversation is beginning to give me a headache."

"After you," Eustice said with a bow.

Jean was waiting by the shed that held the Solexes. He was filling his own with gasoline. "We must buy more petrol so that our return trip will not end in disaster."

"And what about lunch?"

Jean smiled. "You will see a basket on the kitchen table. I was going to bring it after I washed the petrol from my hands."

"Are we going far to the other château?"

"It is about seven kilometers from here, but there are many hills and you would not like to pedal your Solex too far without the help of power."

"I'll agree to that," Eustice said, heading for the kitchen door to get the picnic.

Rachel turned to Jean. "And this other château, is it owned by friends of your parents?"

"Friends in a way. Everyone knows everyone here and the count and countess are kind people, particularly he. But my parents do not socialize too much because of my father's leg that always acts up when he is supposed to go out."

"Antisocial?" Rachel asked.

Jean shrugged. "Hard to say. Perhaps. Or maybe it's just that my father is not a very people person. Did I say that correctly?"

"I got what you meant," Rachel said. "How sad for him."

"My father is not a happy man," Jean agreed. "But I don't know if he doesn't enjoy it a bit. And it does keep my mother near home."

"And is she lonely?"

"She won't ever say so, but I know she is." Jean looked angry for a moment. "Sometimes I see her laughing and suddenly meet my father's look. She will stop as if he'd struck her, and she'll look sad. Sometimes I think I can never forgive him for taking her laughter away."

"That sounds pretty dramatic," Angelica said.

"Maybe it is," Jean agreed. "Maybe I am just at an age where I fight with my father all the time. I have no perspective."

"But I would think your father would be proud of you," Rachel said. "I mean it's not as if you were into drugs or reckless living or anything."

"France is conservative. More than you would think. It would not occur to my father to be proud of me that I am not delinquent. He would like me more obedient."

"What parent wouldn't?" Angelica asked.

"You're right," Jean smiled. "But let's forget all about that and think about the picnic. Why is Byron taking so long to get it together?"

"I'll go see. Where is he?" Angelica went in the kitchen door. "He's not in here and the picnic is sitting on the table." She brought out the basket. Jean took it from her hand and tied it on the back of his Solex.

"Eustice!" Angelica called. "He makes me crazy."

"Here I am." Eustice appeared at the door. "Where's our lunch?"

"Like the rest of us, it's on the Solex ready to go."

"Sorry. Something came up."

"Let's go before Eustice thinks of another excuse." Jean started to pedal down the driveway with

Rachel close behind him. Angelica was getting on her bike when Eustice held her back.

"They were talking in the dining room."

"Who?"

"Who do you think, dummy? The viscount and viscountess!"

"So?"

"So, you should have heard what they were saying!"

"What were they saying then?"

Eustice paused as he slowly kicked up the stand of the Solex. "Well, I got the sense that the viscount was upset about something because he was saying 'But why, Michelle?' and she was speaking so rapidly it was hard to understand her. At first I thought that they were mad at us or at Jean but then he said, 'How could you have saved it all these years? Do you know what this means?' So, I got to thinking that we were on to something a lot more important than us."

"So what?" Angelica looked down the driveway where she could see Rachel and Jean slow down to wait for them. "Come on, Eustice, finish the story before Jean and Rachel leave without us."

"Angelica, be patient!" Eustice glared at her. "The next thing I think he said was 'Michelle, did you do this because of Jean?' And then she said something like 'Jean wasn't even born then' and he said 'So now the Americans arrive and you open it all up again.'" Eustice beamed as he pushed his glasses up his nose. "Wow! How about that?"

Angelica was beginning to get intrigued. "So then what?"

"So then he said something like, 'Why don't you return it to the carriage house now that the children have been forbidden to go there?' And she laughed! She said that she didn't think we would stop going in there and that she had put the book in the best place for it anyway, the library." Eustice looked at Angelica. "We just have to find that book before he makes her destroy it!"

"Why would he do that?"

"Because he said to! And she said no, that it would be important someday for Jean to know the truth."

Rachel came riding up to them, her Solex purring as she circled them. "Any reason for the delay, or is Eustice just taking time off to lecture?"

Eustice grinned. "Yes, there is a reason, and yes, I am taking time off to lecture, so why don't you just go ahead and we'll join you guys later?"

"Who am I to stop the incoming tide? Just make sure you catch up with us before evening!"

Eustice watched her pedal down the road and waited until she was out of earshot before saying with satisfaction. "Well, now at least we know that the mystery is tied up with some book that the viscountess has hidden in the library."

Angelica laughed. "Well, they certainly picked the right place to hide it. Now we know that 'it' is a book in the library. Have you seen the size of their library?"

Eustice spoke quietly. "Listen, I know there is something going on here. I also know that there is a clue either in the carriage house itself or in the form of a book. So we start at the beginning. We look."

"And how are you so sure that if we look we'll come across a mystery?"

"Because of what the viscountess said."

"Which was?"

"She said, 'Roland, we have nothing to fear from the Americans.' And he said, 'You should have destroyed it.'" Eustice's eyes blazed. "If there weren't a mystery, would they worry about us?"

"You have a point. But we'll have to discuss it later or Rachel will kill us. I'm not sure how long she and Jean will wait."

Chapter Three

Rachel and Jean were standing by the road waiting for Eustice and Angelica to catch up to them. Rachel's expression was disapproving but Jean turned to Angelica with a smile. "You will like the Château Menat. In many ways it is lovelier than ours."

Rachel looked at the facade of the château that faced them. "I find that difficult to believe," she said softly. "Your house has such a sense of history."

"As does the Château Menat. Why, it is said that the king of France stayed there!"

Eustice pulled up to them. "Which king?"

"Does it matter? Any old king will impress me,"

Angelica said.

"Angelica, sometimes you're really too American," Eustice remarked.

Rachel suppressed a smile. "Now that you two have kept us waiting, it's up to you to be quiet and let Jean lead the way," she said severely.

"Right-ho, after you." Eustice smiled. "I feel like adventure."

Angelica caught Rachel's glance and grinned. "Can you tell that our bloodhound is onto a scent?"

"Pardon?" Jean looked puzzled.

"Nothing," Eustice said quickly.

"Is he always like this?" Jean laughed.

"Sometimes worse." Rachel started to pedal. "Which way?"

"Right!" Jean cried out. *"À droite!"*

Rachel's engine caught and she moved out of the driveway and into the country road. It was a beautiful summer day and the now familiar sights and smells enhanced the pleasant feel of the wind in her face. She felt rather than saw Jean pull beside her on the road. "You like this country, yes?"

"Oh, very much, yes."

"Then I must tell you something."

Rachel was surprised to see him suddenly look serious. "Tell me whatever you'd like."

Jean shrugged. "It is not a question of like. You

must tell Byron not to be so curious about the carriage house.''

"Why?"

"This I cannot explain. It is a long story of which I only know a small part. But I know that the era during the war was very painful for my parents. Your friend asking questions and bringing it all back again will not make them happy. We could have so much fun with other things this summer.''

"But why don't you tell Eustice this?''

Jean laughed. "I sense that Byron would be only more determined to pursue this investigation. I thought that you being his cousin and his friend might know how to distract him." Jean's voice lowered. "As you certainly could distract me.''

Rachel felt a blush creep to her cheeks. "I'm afraid that if I say anything to Eustice it will have the same effect that your saying something to him would. He is a hard one to discourage.''

"You will try?''

Rachel didn't answer because the beep of a car coming up behind them forced Jean to move ahead of her. She turned her head quickly and caught the eye of Angelica who grinned and raised an eyebrow. Behind her Eustice waved cheerfully, pushing his glasses up his nose and gazing at the beautiful countryside. Rachel slowed up so that she would ride next to him. Angelica passed her and said, "Are you sure you trust me with him?''

"Angelica, stop it!"

"Sorry, Rach."

"To what do I owe this honor?" Eustice smiled at her.

"Companionship."

"Ah."

"Also, Jean has asked me to ask you not to snoop around the carriage house."

"What?"

"That's what I thought you'd say."

"Rachel, what did he say?"

"He just asked me to ask you."

"That's very interesting."

"Well, don't be obvious about the fact that I told you already. I'm supposed to be subtle."

"You never could be subtle with a request like that and you know it."

"That's what I told him."

"Good girl."

"Eustice, you don't think that Jean is hiding something?"

"No, Rach. They are hiding something. He's protecting his parents, and I like him for it."

"He said he didn't really know why his parents are so secretive about the carriage house. He is afraid that your curiosity will agitate them."

"He's probably right," Eustice said softly. "But don't you worry, I won't ruin your summer romance."

"He's not my romance!"

Eustice smiled. "Whatever."

"Here we are, sports fans!" said Angelica, pointing to a large gateway where Jean had turned in.

"What a terrible expression, 'Sports fans.'"

"Eustice, you're worse than Madame Parrot at school."

"Angelica, as I remember, the lady's name was Madame Pierrot."

"That's what I said, *Parrot*."

"*Excusez-moi*, but do you think that you could end your arguing long enough for me to tell you about this château?" Jean had stopped his bike and stood with one foot on the ground at the gate of the Château Menat. Jean pointed. "You see, there are the tennis courts and already they are playing without us."

"Thank heavens."

"Byron, I detect a distinct lack of, what's the word—*enthusiasm*?"

They all rode down the driveway and turned off to go toward the court. Rachel could see that there were four people around her own age playing. As they heard the Solexes approaching they stopped and turned toward them.

"Jean!" A very pretty dark-haired girl waved. *"Viens ici!"*

"Sabine, *ça va*?" Jean stopped and got off his Solex in time to catch the dark-haired girl in a hug. He kissed both her cheeks. Rachel felt her heart sink.

"Jean, you must meet our guests!"

"And you must meet ours, Sabine."

Sabine turned and Rachel could see that she was very pretty in a gypsy kind of way. Her dark curls were caught up in a bright-red headband and brown eyes danced as they looked at Jean. Already she had the continental beauty that Rachel felt separated the Europeans from the Americans. She hadn't yet figured out what the secret was to the relaxed sensuousness that seemed to be a French characteristic even from an early age, but whatever it was Sabine had it. It was hard not to dislike her immediately. However, her warmth was disarming as she rushed up immediately to Rachel and said, "I am Sabine and you must forgive me for only greeting Jean. I have not seen him in over a year now and we are childhood friends."

"Of course."

Eustice came over then. Rachel could see that her cousin had already noticed Sabine's beauty. He had whisked off his glasses and blinked to focus his gaze on her. "We are also childhood friends." He waved toward Rachel and Angelica. "Rachel is my cousin and Angelica has known me all my life."

Sabine smiled and continued the introductions. "Jack over there only arrived from London yesterday. His partner, Hans, is from Berlin. Manuel, that dark-haired boy, is from Barcelona." The boys smiled and waved to the Americans.

"So," Sabine said brightly, "shall we play some tennis?"

"Not for me, thanks." Eustice pulled a book out of his pocket. "I hate to make a bad impression on a first meeting."

"By not playing tennis?" Jack asked.

"By playing abysmal tennis," Eustice answered.

"And you have four already," Jean said. "We will watch you."

Sabine shook her head. "We will play round-robin with one of us leaving after we serve and another coming in. Then we will all get to play and talk with one another too!"

The morning passed quickly and pleasantly with everyone but Eustice playing tennis. It must have been close to noon when a gray-haired lady came down the path carrying soft drinks in a basket. "I thought you all might be thirsty," she said. "Sabine, you must allow your guests a break!"

"Of course I will, *Maman*."

"As a matter of fact, I think I've had enough exercise," Eustice said as he got up to grab a soft drink. "Heavy reading can make a man pretty thirsty," he said to the countess.

Jack moved over next to Angelica. "Your friend is quite a wit, isn't he?"

"Nitwit is more the word."

Jack laughed, his blue eyes catching Angelica's.

Jean smiled. "But we can keep Monsieur Byron in line, no?"

"No," Angelica said. "But we can have fun trying."

"And who is Byron if I may ask?" Sabine inquired.

"I'm embarrassed to say that it's me," Eustice said crossly.

"But you said your name was Eustice!"

"So I did."

Jean laughed. "Okay, okay. I will not tease Byron any more if he doesn't like it . . ." He smiled at Eustice. "But I honestly think that it is a more attractive name."

"Coming from you it sounds fine, but from anyone else it sounds silly."

"I like it too," Sabine said, her dark eyes studying Eustice carefully. "Yes, I think it suits you."

"You do?"

"Oui," she said firmly. "You are tall and very thin with those very lovely eyes, yes, I think you are romantic looking."

Rachel could see Eustice was at a loss for words. The color rose to his cheeks but the look he gave Sabine was not shy. "Thank you," he said seriously.

Sabine smiled. "I admit that I, too, love to read. But why are you trying to read without your glasses, Byron?"

Eustice's blush deepened as he pulled his glasses out of his pocket. "They do make it easier," he agreed.

"Let me see them on you," Sabine continued, and as Eustice put them on and gazed at her through the thick lenses, she laughed.

"I think you look *très chic*, Monsieur Byron." Turning to the others she said, "Don't you all agree?"

"I do," Rachel said.

Jean grinned. "She's right, Byron."

Angelica sipped her soft drink and gave a quick glance at Jack. "Let's explore a bit. Does this path lead to your house, Sabine?"

"Château," Sabine corrected.

Angelica shrugged. "Whatever."

Sabine laughed. "Forgive me if I sounded a little snobbish about my home. We French are very proud of our heritage."

"So you should be," Eustice said. "I've read quite a bit about your culture and I found—"

Angelica ignored him and, with Jack close behind her, followed Sabine down the lovely winding path that led from the tennis courts to the château. Eustice and Rachel trailed after them.

"You see that they lined the path with natural wildflowers," Sabine said. "And the main château is just over the hill."

"No wonder so many artists have lived in this country," Eustice said, looking out over the fields. "It's so beautiful."

"It is lovely," Jack said. "But no more so, for example, than the English Lake District."

Sabine glared. "That is not so."

"Spain has the most lovely coast in Europe," Manuel said from behind her.

"And Germany has the Alps!" Rachel glanced back at Hans who smiled at her gratefully.

"Yes," he continued. "And in the wintertime you cannot find a more beautiful country in the world."

"Except for the good old U.S.A.," Eustice said.

"But yours is a naive country." Sabine shook her head. "You all do not understand the rest of the world because you are all so isolated on your large rich land."

"What do you mean by that?" Rachel asked.

Jean's dark eyes clouded. "You see, we who live in Europe must deal with other countries and cultures constantly because we are all so small. But in the United States it is different. You don't have to learn other languages or accept other cultures."

"That's not true," Eustice said. "The United States has many different cultures and minorities and we all must learn to live together."

"But you all live together as Americans," Jean said. "We who live on the continent of Europe share a small space as different peoples."

"There is the château now," Sabine interrupted, pointing to a large and astonishingly lovely house that loomed ahead of them.

"All this land is yours?" Angelica asked incredulously.

"Most of it still is."

"Was your house occupied during the war too?"

Sabine gave Jack a quick glance. "All of the large houses were occupied by the German army during the Second World War."

"But your mother is so young." Rachel turned to Jean. "Was she also there?"

"My mother was then a young girl," Jean said carefully. "She is my father's second wife."

"He was divorced?" Angelica asked.

"No. My father's first wife died."

"And your mother is from around here?"

"You're awfully curious sometimes, Byron, do you know that?"

Eustice blushed. "I'm sorry, Jean. I didn't mean to pry, really. I am a nosy American. It's just that we have never actually been anywhere near the war. It kind of brings it home to us."

Jean laughed. "I understand. It's just that I get so sick of hearing about the war. Of course it all happened a generation before I was born, but my father is of that generation. I see its effects on him even though I never knew what he was like before the Germans came."

"What effects?" Rachel asked.

Jean shrugged. "It's hard to be specific. He is so proud and closemouthed about it. My mother is affected the most and perhaps this is why it all bothers me so much. No one really talks about it, but it's always there. I feel it."

"Yes," Sabine agreed. "My parents are also this way. They were children during the war and protected somewhat by the fact that the Germans wanted the families of the châteaus to seem eager to help Hitler's army for propaganda purposes. But they will not speak of their parents and why they were spared from the full effects of the occupation."

"Was there a Resistance group here?" Eustice asked.

"I am sure of it," Jean said. "But whenever I ask, my parents insist that I close the subject." He paused. "Which means that my father had nothing to do with the Resistance."

"But you weren't around," Rachel said.

"So I will never know," Jean said sadly.

"Look, let's make a pact," Eustice said. "The rule should be that if we dig up any information by exploring your barn, Jean, or if we unearth anything bad, we go right to you for your okay."

"Okay about what?" Sabine asked.

"Okay to pursue it further."

"Pursue what further?" Jean sounded annoyed.

Eustice sat down and put a long piece of grass into his mouth. "The story," he said. "The story that is still making your mother lock us out of the carriage house forty years after the war. The story that is making your father nervous, Jean. The story that hangs over you like a cloud, man."

"Aren't you curious as to why we can't explore the carriage house?" Angelica asked.

"The roof is weak," Jean persisted stubbornly.

"That excuse is weak," Eustice said.

"But what if—" Jean sounded uncertain.

"What if what?" Rachel asked him gently.

"What if we find out something bad? I don't want to hurt my mother. And I won't let you hurt her either."

"Eustice maybe you've gone a little too far," Rachel said. "These things are none of our business."

"I hear you, Rach," Eustice said quietly. To Jean he added, "I'm a history buff and I can never resist an unanswered question. It's in my blood. But I will do what you say."

Jean sat down on the grass. "You know," he began, "I guess I have always wanted to know what happened then."

"But, are you willing to let us look into this?" Eustice asked.

"May we just go step by step?" Jean asked. "May I have the option to stop your search if it goes too far?"

"Are you that positive that we're going to find something bad?" Rachel asked.

Jean's dark eyes seemed almost liquid with feeling as they met hers. "Yes," he whispered.

Sabine sat down next to him and put her arm around him.

Angelica cleared her throat. "Don't you think that we've discussed this enough? I say we go into the château, take a look around, and see how we feel about all this later."

"Which means that you still will have the opportunity to stop us from investigating, Jean."

Jean gave Eustice a long, penetrating look. "I think that I won't stop you. I think that perhaps I have always wanted to unearth some of the answers you seek. Because of my mother, I have not had the courage. But we will protect her, won't we? She will not suffer from this? Can we make that the only rule?"

"It certainly sounds like a fair one to me," Eustice said.

Jean stood up and smiled at him. "Byron, I think you and I have many things to learn together this summer."

Eustice nodded solemnly. "I only hope that I can be as brave as you are."

Jean's face tightened for an instant. "I only hope we find out the whole truth."

"That's why we're going to need all the help we can get. Is everyone willing to help us?" Eustice asked.

"Sounds okay to me," Angelica said.

"Then count me in," Jack said.

"And me," Sabine said, leaning over to ruffle Jean's hair.

"And us," Manuel said, smiling at Hans, who nodded eagerly.

"I just wonder—" Angelica began.

"Wonder what?"

"I just wonder when we'll have time to learn French?"

Chapter Four

"Where is everybody?"

"Eustice, you've been prowling around all morning. Why don't you let us be? I'm trying to write a letter home that will convince my parents that I am actually learning some French this summer."

"How are you going to do that, Angelica?" Eustice, looking bored, was wandering around the room opening and closing drawers.

Angelica looked up at him from where she was lying on her bed. "This," she said, holding up a large French-English dictionary. "I'm writing the entire letter in French to impress them."

"Do they read French?" Rachel asked.

"Of course not, that's why it doesn't really matter whether I'm grammatically correct or not. They'd just be impressed that I'm writing in another language."

"There's Sabine!" Eustice ran from the window out the door. "Get Jean and tell them that the kids from Château Menat have arrived at last!"

"I hear you, Byron." Jean strolled down the hall toward him.

"Let's go, man!"

"*Mon Dieu*, Byron is so serious today. All this activity and excitement about a picnic?"

"Hardly." Rachel smiled. "Don't you see? Now we can play Sardines!"

"Ah, that explains it perfectly. All this excitement so we can play hide-and-seek?"

"Well . . . not exactly. I'll explain later."

Eustice laughed. "Come on! Let's go meet them!"

Rachel smiled. "I think his plan is to initiate a large game of Sardines so that if your parents ask why we are hiding in some unlikely place, like the carriage house, we have an alibi."

"Alibi is the wrong word. We have a cover, Rach."

"Nit-picking again," Angelica muttered.

Eustice leaned over and snatched her letter out of her hand and as Angelica howled and lunged for it, he skipped away from her and read:

"*Chère Maman and Papa*. Oh, Angelica this is cute!"

"I'm warning you, Byron."

"*Je having a très bon time ici en France avec many nice enfants.*"

"If anyone in this room laughs I'm pushing them out the window."

"Then don't read any more Eustice, I can't bear it!" Rachel told him.

"Courage, Rachel, there's more."

"Our guests are here, Eustice, weren't you just going out to greet them?"

"*Eustice is toujours un pain in the bon-bon, but Rachel is toujours wonderful et I am having a bon time ice.*"

"Ice?" Jean tried to keep his mouth from twitching.

"I didn't write 'ice.' Eustice is just being mean."

"*Ici.* You're right. It isn't ice."

"Thank you. May I now have my letter back?"

Eustice shut his eyes and handed it back to her. "I hate to do this, it's so *you*, Angelica. But listen, I'll make a deal with you."

"Yeah? What kind of deal?"

"Don't sound so suspicious. If you let me read it, I'll go over it with you and help you correct some of your grammar."

"You will? Without laughing at me?"

Eustice met Jean's laughing glance. "I'll try not to, is that fair enough?"

"I'll think about it. Maybe Rachel can give me better terms."

Madame appeared from nowhere looking beautiful and serene in her silk housedress. "I think you have guests waiting downstairs for you." She gave Jean a questioning look.

"Yes, *Maman*, we have invited them for a picnic."

Her smile lit her face. "How lovely. And will you give them something to eat?"

"Danielle and I have organized a picnic. I rode to the village this morning for some cheese and sausage and fruit and Danielle got two extra baguettes."

"Hey, man, I would have helped you do that if you had told me."

"Byron, *mon ami*, you were too busy in your book this morning."

"Eustice is always too busy in his books, you should learn to ignore that, Jean. We do."

"After that letter, Angelica, I'm not surprised."

Madame laughed. "Please! Your guests must be wondering where you are." Her eyes softened as they looked at Eustice. "You will not argue with your friend any more this morning, yes? The viscount is resting and we must not have angry voices disturb him, *s'il vous plaît*!"

"Of course, Madame, whatever you say."

She smiled and left the room. Eustice's eyes followed her out.

"Your mother is a beauty, Jean."

"Yes, she is." Jean gave him a quick sharp look. "We will be careful not to hurt her, won't we?"

Eustice put his hands on Jean's shoulders. "I never would want to do anything to hurt so beautiful a lady, ever. Do you believe me?"

"Yes."

"Then let's find out what happened forty years ago that makes her still frightened about the carriage house."

"Do you really think she is frightened, Eustice?" Jean asked.

"Why would she put a new lock on the carriage house door? Why would she be so concerned about our exploring it and, most important, what was she carrying the other night only minutes after warning us not to go in there at all?"

"All right." Jean headed out the door with a final smile. "We go to play hide-and-seek."

"I've always loved the game myself," Eustice said brightly and followed him out. "You girls just come on down as soon as you've completed your all-French letters home. Try to make it this century."

Angelica slowly got off her bed and stretched. "Why hasn't he told Jean about the conversation he overheard between the viscount and viscountess?"

"He will when the right time comes," Rachel said. "I think that he's trying to gather as much concrete information as he can before he puts it on the table for Jean."

"Maybe," Angelica agreed. "And maybe he wants to play Sardines to have some cozy time with Sabine."

"Maybe, but I don't think so. I think that we are not going to say much to the kids from Château Menat either."

"But did you see Eustice's face when Sabine said he was cute with his glasses?" Angelica gave Rachel a sly look. "That makes two of you with French romances."

The sharpness of her tone made Rachel stop at the door and turn around. "Are you missing Peter, Angelica?"

"A lot."

"I thought so. There was a sad look on your face at the tennis court yesterday when Sabine was complimenting Eustice."

"Let's forget it."

"Angelica! Rachel! Move your butts!"

They heard Sabine downstairs ask, "Butts? *Qu'est-que c'est* butts?"

Angelica grinned.

They heard Eustice respond as they walked into the front hall where the kids from Château Menat were standing around waiting for them.

"Butts, er, are backsides, Sabine. You know." A blush crept up his cheeks. Sabine's eyes danced. "*Mais non*, I do not understand backside."

Angelica laughed. "You know, Sabine, I'm going to like you."

"Yes. This will be a good summer. I feel it."

"Can we play now or are we all just going to stand here saying how much we like each other?"

"Then let's go." Jack waved Hans and Manuel out the door after Eustice and Jean. He gave a quick look toward Angelica. "Is this going to be safe?"

"One thing you never know about Eustice," Angelica responded. "You never know whether it will be safe or whether it will be legal. Otherwise he's as steady as a rock."

"Blimey!"

Manuel laughed. "When Jack starts sounding like a real Cockney, we should worry."

"When Eustice wants us to play simple games like hide-and-seek we should all worry."

"Well, Miss Angelica, it sure sounds as if we could spend a lot of this summer worrying."

"I've done it before."

"Okay, everybody stop talking. Let's get down to business."

Eustice stood in the middle as they all surrounded him. "You all know how to play Sardines, right? One person hides and then the others look for him.

When they find him they hide with him and the last person to find everyone is 'it' next.''

Sabine grinned. ''It sounds a lot like the French game of Sardines.''

''And the German game of Sardines.''

''And the Spanish game of—''

''Is everyone having fun this morning? Shall we all just sit down and get all this wit and merriment out of our systems?''

''Hey, you can dish it out but you can't take it.'' Jack grinned.

''I assume you are 'it,' Bryon.''

''That's right, Jean. So you guys go back into the front hall there and count to a hundred. No, make it two hundred.''

''We'll make it one hundred. If we count to two hundred you could fly back to the States.''

''Or you could make Angelica count in French to five. That would take about the same amount of time. Come on, let's get going!''

Eustice ran from their midst and they could hear him for a moment on the driveway that led to the back of the château. They all began to count slowly. Rachel looked around the group from one to another. Jack with his lean looks was the least handsome, although his face showed more character. His eyes were sharp and glanced around to the others constantly before they came to rest on Angelica standing next to him. Poor Jack. It would be hard to distract Angelica from her boyfriend at home, Peter de Vere. Meeting Sabine's friendly smile, Rachel thought she caught a look of comprehension as Sabine's dark eyes moved from Jean to herself. As she felt the blood rush to her cheeks she felt the cool look of Hans studying her. He was the tallest of the boys, standing close to six feet with clean blond looks that contrasted with Manuel's Latin features. All in all, they were an unusual group, she thought. In spite of their different origins, she felt a sense of closeness to them all, especially now that they were all working on a common cause.

"I'm bored. Do we have to count any more?"

"Angelica, we've only counted to forty."

"That's enough. He'll never know."

"I suggest that we split up," Jean said. "Sabine, you take Jack toward the barn. Manuel and Hans, you go and check the hay field. Rachel and Angelica and I will look near the house."

"Right."

"But Jean," Rachel whispered as the others moved off, "Jean, we *know* where he's hiding."

"Yes, but we need time to explore, before the others discover what we're up to."

"You mean to keep it secret from the others?" Angelica asked him.

"For now, yes." Jean looked serious. "That's what Byron wanted. Let's split up and each go to the carriage house separately. He must have figured out how to get in by now. See you there.''

Rachel wasted time wandering near the kitchen, looking as if she were involved in the hunt but actually waiting until Angelica and Jean had been out of sight for a while. Then she moved around the house and inconspicuously moved toward the carriage house. Going past the door she saw the new padlock remained untouched, so she moved toward the back out of sight from the château. At first she saw no possible way to get in and was just beginning to feel despair when she heard a slight ''Hsst!'' and saw that a board had been loosened and a small opening made for her. One finger came out and gestured for her to come in. It looked so silly she chuckled.

''Rachel, stop laughing and get in here before the others see!''

She quickly crouched down and crawled through the tiny space. Someone pulled her all the way in and she stood up, rubbing her eyes. ''How did you guys find this so fast?''

''Eustice whistled.''

''Subtle.''

''Effective. Rach, you should be proud of me.''

''As soon as I see you, I'm sure I will be.''

As her vision cleared she saw Angelica, Eustice and Jean smiling at her. ''Did anyone have the sense to bring a flashlight?''

"Rachel, do you take me for an idiot?"

"Well . . ."

"Quit kidding! Look over here and see what I found!"

They followed Eustice toward the main mural at the rear. There was a huge woman dressed in uniform holding a machine gun and hovering over what appeared to be verse in German.

"What do you think it says?" Angelica asked.

"Propaganda, I'm sure."

"Yes, but that's not what I was looking at, Jean." He pointed to a hole in the wall. "Look at that!"

"As I remember there are a lot of those holes about," Jean said.

"And did you guess what they were? Did you?"

"Can you ever just come out and say what you're thinking?" Angelica sounded impatient.

"I'm thinking bullet holes, Angelica. And a lot of them."

"Yes, but I knew that."

"You what?"

Jean looked uncomfortable. "They have always been there."

"But why didn't you say so? Don't you think that they might be important to our investigation?"

"I don't know."

Eustice cast a frustrated look at Rachel. "Are we going in circles?"

"No, Byron, I am sorry. Let me try to explain."

Eustice sat down on the ground. "We've got plenty of time."

Jean sat down. "You see? I told you. Bits and pieces are all there are. How will we ever find out the whole story? It cannot be done."

"Now, wait a minute. You haven't even started yet. Tell me what you know and at least let us try to sort this out."

"Yes, you're right." Jean met his gaze. "I don't know much, but I know that when the Allies were liberating France the section of the army centered here decided to destroy everything. Revenge? Spite? I don't know. The villagers, perhaps the local branch of the Resistance, found out and decided to help my family save the château. Some of them were caught. And from what I gather, they were executed."

"Here?" Angelica's voice was hoarse.

Jean nodded. "That's what Sabine's mother said. She was not here but she heard."

"And your father? What does he say?"

"My father will not discuss the war."

"But he was in it, wasn't he?"

Jean nodded. "He was an officer in the village government."

"Under the Nazis?" Rachel asked.

Jean's head lowered. "I guess so," he said sadly.

"So your father collaborated with those murderers?"

"Angelica, take it easy!"

Jean raised his head and met Eustice's gaze. "I have never had the courage to investigate further. To confirm—"

"Confirm?" Eustice asked tentatively.

"Confirm that my father was part of all that."

"Oh, Jean." Rachel touched his arm.

"I don't need your sympathy. We cannot know what it was like, what they were like. I am sure that my father had a reason."

"No wonder you never felt like going any further with this," Eustice said.

Jean nodded. "And yet, if we continue, maybe we will find out."

"Find out what your father did?"

"Find out why he was a traitor."

"*Alors!* Here you are!" Sabine's head popped through the opening. "Very clever indeed!" She scrambled through the opening and joined them. "The others may have seen me," she said.

"I think it's time you told him what you overheard, Eustice," Rachel said firmly.

"*Excusez-moi*, but what are you all talking about? Is this not Sardines?"

Jean ignored Sabine's question. "What did you hear?"

"Your mother has hidden a book in the library," Eustice said. "I overheard her talking to your father. It has to do with the war. And I think it is the key to what we're looking for."

Sabine interrupted. "What is in the book? Why do I feel as if I'm missing something?"

They heard the others outside and as the board slipped back they could see Jack's face.

"Listen, mates, I couldn't fit through there if I tried and old Hans here could do himself some damage. How about coming out and helping us find some lunch?"

"Good idea," Angelica said, leading the way. "Come, Sabine, I'll explain what's going on; you'll never get Eustice down to earth enough to tell you. He'll be like this for hours now. Trust me."

As the others made their way out Rachel waited for Jean. He didn't move for a while so she went back to sit next to him. "Is this going to cause you too much pain, Jean? I can always ask Eustice to stop."

"Stop what?" Jean asked her. "Stop me from finding out the truth about my father? I don't know. I feel as if I couldn't stop this if I wanted to."

"Because Eustice is so persistent?"

"No, because I think that all my life I have hidden. I think it will be better to know it all. It's just that I know it will be more than just my father's secrets that may come out. My mother has secrets too and they are all intertwined with his. I know this." He took her hand. "And Rachel, I'm frightened."

Chapter Five

"Eustice, you can't just walk in there!"

"What are you talking about, Angelica? That was the plan."

"I know, but Jean hasn't given us the 'all clear' yet. What if Madame forgot something?"

"She's right, Eustice, come back out and wait until Jean says it's okay."

Eustice turned from the door to the master chamber and looked at Rachel and Angelica grimly. "What's the matter with you two all of a sudden?"

"Nothing's the matter with us. It's only that we are about to search the private library of our hostess without her knowledge or her son being there. That's almost breaking and entering.''

"What do you mean by breaking and entering, Angelica? We *live* here."

"You know what I mean."

Jean came down the long wide hallway toward them. His dark eyes were bright with excitement. "She has gone," he whispered, "and Papa is reading in the garden. We are safe."

"For a while at least," Rachel said. "And your father won't pop in on us?"

Jean looked down at her. "If my father were to return, we would hear him huffing up the stairs for hours before he came into sight. His leg gives him so much pain, he tries not to climb the stairs any more than necessary."

"Are you guys going to come in here and help me out or are you going to chitchat all day out there?"

"Byron, you're an impatient detective, *n'est-ce pas?*"

"Well, there's something about searching a room that gives a guy the jitters, you know what I mean?"

Jean grinned. "I think I'm about to."

Rachel followed him into the master bedroom. She stopped a moment to admire it. The great long room had obviously been built in another era. Beautiful paintings hung everywhere except over the master bed where there was a large, obviously valuable tapestry. On closer inspection Rachel could see that the ornate furniture was broken and chipped. The chintz on the chairs was worn and in spots, torn. But the proportions of the room and the grandeur of the pieces made all of them fall silent for an instant.

"My goodness," Rachel breathed. "This is their bedroom?"

"Yes, of course, why are you surprised?"

"Because it looks like a museum. There's no clutter."

"You wish my parents to be messy?"

"Of course not, but there's no stuff that would make you think someone lived here."

Jean burst out laughing. "That is true enough. But come, let me show you the entire layout of their suite here."

He led them through another door on the other side of the bedroom which was obviously Madame's dressing room. The walls were covered with mirrors and lined with closets and drawers. Rachel gazed in awe at the rococo dressing table and the matching mirror, framed in gold with cupids and flowers carved into the wood. On either side of the mirror was a large frame; one held a photograph of the viscount as a much younger man, and the other was of Jean perhaps only a year or two younger.

"What a handsome man your father was," Rachel said. "He still is, of course, but in this photograph his face is gentler somehow."

Jean nodded. "Yes, I see that. Sometimes when his leg doesn't hurt so much and we are together, I see that expression. But mostly, I see it when he looks at my mother."

"But he loves you, Jean."

Jean shrugged. "Perhaps. He is so formal a man, it is hard for him to show his feelings. This is why he loves my mother so much. She is very open and loving."

"How did they meet?"

"It was during the war. My father's first wife was killed. I don't know how but I think it was during a bombing. My mother was very young and she came to work at the château for my father. I suppose he must have fallen in love with her right away, but he didn't marry her until years after the war was over."

"I wonder why?"

"My mother had to finish school and then she went to college. My father paid her way through, I know. But she once told me that he wanted to make sure that her love was not that of a grateful schoolgirl. He waited for her to be old enough to know her own mind."

"Then they were married," Rachel said. "How romantic. But you weren't born for many years."

"Yes. And I wonder if my father really wanted a young son to compete for her love." Jean looked down at Rachel. "Is that a terrible thing to say?"

"No, of course it isn't," Rachel said softly, "but I am sure that it is not true."

"Oh, Rachel, I hope not!"

Rachel was about to continue the conversation when she remembered they were on a mission. They had to move quickly to find the book and already she could hear Eustice exploring the other rooms. She would have to pick up on this conversation later and convince Jean that his father was proud of him. How could he not appreciate such a fine son?

Eustice's voice cut into her thoughts. "Look in here! It's like a tiny den!"

Rachel followed Jean into the book-lined library. There was a fireplace here, too, and the long windows looked out over the gardens in back, as did the master bedroom. The library was far more casually furnished than the bedroom—a few deep chairs, a couple of scarred tables, and an old couch with sagging springs. Books were scattered comfortably about and Madame's sewing was set up near the windows to catch the light.

"Now this is more like it," Eustice said. "I could live here."

"My parents essentially do in the winter," Jean said.

"I can see why. They've got everything right here." Eustice sat down in one of the large easy chairs. "A man could get used to it."

"Stop playing, Eustice, we have to get going!"

"Is there a safe anywhere?" Eustice looked around. "This room is just made for a safe or a secret passage. Any secret passages, Jean?"

"Not that I know of, Byron, but I wouldn't be surprised if you found one."

"Do we even know what we're looking for?" Angelica sounded tired.

"Giving up already?"

"Of course not," she snapped, "but let's get this over with."

"I agree," Rachel said. "I don't like being in here. I feel as if I were invading your parents' privacy."

"Okay. What we're looking for is a small book."

"Big help," Angelica muttered, looking at the book-lined walls.

"Why don't we each take a quarter of the room and look?" Jean suggested. "Maybe the clue will leap out at one of us."

"Just look at these wonderful old books in their original bindings!" Rachel said. "There are so many of them and they look as if they should be in a museum."

"Much of this house could be a museum," Jean said.

"Look at the dust on them," Angelica said. "This is probably the oldest dust I've ever been around."

"Napoleonic dust!" Rachel laughed.

"But that's it!" Eustice pushed his glasses up his nose. "We look for a book *without* the dust!"

"Great clue, Eustice; that narrows it down to maybe half the room."

"That's better than nothing."

"Here's a box, kind of tucked away. I don't think there's any dust on it either."

"Rachel, you angel! And see! It's almost out of reach!" Eustice crowed.

Rachel couldn't reach the box so Jean came over and gently pulled it out of the shelf, leaving one of the books leaning out so they would know where to put it. The box was made of faded red leather and as Jean tried to open it he gave Eustice a glance. "Perhaps you would like to do this, Byron?"

"Not at all, man, this is your house and this is your mystery. We're just lending a hand."

The box didn't open. "Locked!" Jean's face was crestfallen. "We won't even know if this is what we're looking for!"

"Of course it's what we're looking for. It's locked, isn't it?"

"Someone's coming!" Rachel cried. "I hear your father Jean! He is huffing and moaning on the stairs!"

"Put it back quickly!"

"But we have to see what's inside!"

"Byron, it must wait. We will find the key. It must be somewhere in my mother's room. But now we put the box back!"

"No!"

"Eustice, this is Jean's house and he makes the rules."

"Rachel, if we leave the box here, we can't make sure it will still be here when we get the chance to come back. What if Jean's father sees that the den has been searched?"

"He won't. We haven't left any evidence," Eustice said.

"Hurry!" Rachel cried.

"Jean, we can't leave this here! This is our master clue!"

Jean's lips tightened as Eustice looked at him pleadingly.

"Oh dear, where shall we go?" Rachel asked.

Jean caught her arm. "You don't have to worry, we can slip out, but you have to follow me." Jean turned to Eustice who was still holding the red box under his arm.

"Well?" Eustice asked him.

"Okay. We take the box." Jean pulled it out of Eustice's hands and smiled. "If my father does see us, he may as well think that I took it. Otherwise, he will get even more angry."

Rachel turned to Eustice angrily. "See what you're doing with your endless mysteries? You have no feelings for what Jean may face if they find the box is missing!"

Jean touched her hand. "Hush, we will discuss this later." He turned and led the way out of the den toward his mother's dressing room. "My father won't come this way. He will come through his own dressing room on the other side."

"So what do we do now?"

"We wait, Byron, for him to pass this room. Then we sneak through the bedroom and out that way. He will probably go right into the den."

They could hear the viscount come down the hall. His stiffness was apparent. With each step they could hear a low groan of pain. They stood as still as mice as he moved by and eventually they heard him entering the den, just as Jean had predicted. Soundlessly, Jean gestured for the others to follow. He slowly opened the door to the master bedroom. The box was tucked tightly under his arm as he led the way back into the long hallway. They could hear the viscount moving about the den as they scurried along the hall and back down the long stairway. They didn't stop to say a word until they had reached the servants' quarters. Rachel could sense Jean's discomfort.

"Oh, look what we've made you do!" she cried. "I will take the box back as soon as your father leaves. I promise! No matter what Eustice says!" She turned to glare at her cousin. "Sometimes, you're incredibly insensitive."

"Rachel—"

"I mean it. Eustice, sometimes you're so greedy for a story you'll let yourself walk all over the feelings of others!"

"Hush, Rachel, you exaggerate." Jean's hand reached for hers. "Yes, it is a little frightening, but Byron here is making me face something I have never had the courage to face, no?"

Eustice put a hand on his shoulder. "You know, Jean, she has a point. I go crazy over mysteries or any kind of puzzle for that matter. I'm sorry. I'll take this back if you want." He picked up the box from where Jean had placed it on Angelica's bureau. "Just say the word and back it goes."

Jean smiled at him. "Without finding the key, Byron?"

Eustice grinned at him. "See, Rachel? We're dealing with a hero here."

Rachel smiled at Jean. "Yes, we are. I just hope that's what he wants to be."

Jean bowed. "What man can resist an opportunity to impress a lovely girl?"

"So, Eustice, how do you plan to go about finding the key?" Angelica asked impatiently.

"We just might have to break it," Jean said.

"Then your mother is sure to find out we've tampered with it!" Rachel shook her head. "I won't let you do that—at least not until we've tried everything else."

"How about a bobby pin?" Angelica asked. "That's what they do in spy movies."

"You're brilliant sometimes." Eustice beamed. "But how do we get a bobby pin?"

"Who in this room has the long dark hair?"

"You do, Angelica, but—"

"But my mother always packs bobby pins because she hates my hair in my face." Angelica grinned. "I never use them. Look!" She reached into her top drawer and pulled out a box. "See?"

"Great!" Eustice grabbed them from her hand.

He peeled the tips of the bobby pins and gently inserted one into the tiny keyhole. "See. No breaks, no mess, no problem."

"It looks like a journal or something," Rachel commented.

"Maybe a log of some sort," Eustice agreed.

"It's in German," Jean said, looking over his shoulder.

"And it's old," Angelica whispered.

"Why would my mother hide this in the carriage house all these years?" As Jean's hands passed over the faded leather binding, his puzzled expression met Eustice's.

"Can you read German?" Eustice asked him.

"A little." Jean shrugged.

"You mean after all this we have a clue that we can't understand?"

"For the moment, Byron, yes."

Eustice shut his eyes and fell back onto Rachel's bed. "I'm going to scream."

"That won't be necessary," Jean laughed. "I have an idea."

Eustice sat up. "Yeah? Thank heaven someone has."

"There is a man in the village who speaks German. He was a hero in the Resistance but now he is the custodian of the school on the other side of Trange. He works mostly in the library there. *He* will tell us what this is."

"And when can we go to him?"

"The sooner the better. If this is what my mother was so careful to hide from us, then she will notice if it is gone."

"Then let's put the box back and keep the book."

"A good idea, Byron. I will do that this afternoon."

"When your mother has returned?" Eustice looked doubtful.

"When my father has left for his walk and my mother naps. They will not notice if I go in and out of their den."

"Would you like me to go with you, Jean?"

"Not this time, Byron." Jean smiled at him. "But thanks just the same."

At dinner that evening Jean crept in a bit late and gave them the thumbs-up.

Rachel glanced over at the viscount and viscountess but they hadn't noticed. Angelica quickly began to attempt to speak to them in French and the surprise on their faces made Eustice shout with laughter. The viscountess frowned at him and then her face broke into a smile as she quickly shot a glance at her husband. "You must not tease your friend for trying to speak French with us. It is the best way for her to get better at it."

"Yes, I know, Madame, but we all would understand it so much better if she just spoke in English!"

"Eustice, you make it sound as if you're Mr. Fluent."

"Next to you, Angelica, anyone would be."

"*Mes enfants!* Do you never stop this fighting?"

Jean laughed. "Don't try, *Maman*, it is not worth it. First of all, they do not stop this fighting and second of all, they enjoy it, no?"

"No." Angelica looked at Rachel. "You tell them."

"No," Rachel said, smiling.

Jean's eyes lit up as they met hers. "But then, *Maman*, you forgot that Rachel appears sweet and pretty, but she too loves to fight. This must be the American way."

"Just with good friends, Jean." Eustice smiled at the viscountess. "You see? It is our way to show affection."

The viscount frowned. "Would it be possible for us either to continue this conversation in the proper language or cease to speak at all?"

"*Oui*, Papa." Jean shot the others a look, and silence descended upon the table.

Chapter Six

Do you have the book?"

"Yes, Byron, I have the book." Jean patted his back and smiled at Eustice. "Don't be so nervous. They haven't even noticed that it's missing."

"Yet."

"But why would they suspect that it is gone?"

Eustice shrugged. "Your mother is a very perceptive woman. If she was careful to move the box from the carriage house to their study, she must be sensitive about that book. And if she's sensitive about that book, who's to say that she won't check and make sure it's still there every day!"

"He's got a point, Jean," Rachel said as she got on her Solex.

"Then we must hurry and get it translated." Jean started his bike. "Which is where we are now going."

"Who is this guy again?"

"Father Thomas. He runs the library at the local school. He is a historian of sorts and will know what this means."

"We hope," Angelica said. "Otherwise Eustice will make life miserable for us all."

"Angelica, aren't you interested in this?" Eustice pushed his glasses up his nose. "I mean this could be something important. We know the book was from the war and that it's important to Jean's parents. Don't you think it could be something cool?"

Angelica shrugged. "Maybe. And maybe it's too cool."

"What do you mean by that?"

"That maybe it's none of our business and it will bring trouble."

Eustice looked over at Jean. "You certainly have a vote in this. But don't you think that we should at least try to find out what this means? And if the answer is too big for us we just put the book back and forget it. Is that fair?"

Rachel laughed.

"What's that laugh mean, Cousin?"

"It means that I don't believe you could ever stop pursuing a case if it interests you."

"Just watch me. I don't want Jean hurt by any of this. I know his parents are involved in this somehow. This time, I mean it."

"Byron, even I don't believe you."

"That's because you don't want to, do you?" Eustice raised his voice over the sound of his Solex. "You're just as curious as we are, even though you have more at stake."

"Perhaps you are right." Jean's mouth tightened and he accelerated suddenly, shooting ahead of them. "Just follow me and we will soon know how good a clue you found us."

The small town of Trange could be passed through in the blink of an eye. A small grocery store, a post office, a seedy café took up one side of the street, and on the other was the school. Several of the older locals were sitting at the café looking as if they had been there all day and even perhaps all year. Above, on the second floor, Rachel could see women hanging their laundry out to dry from the windows. She parked her Solex behind Jean's and followed him into the dank and mildewed library. Sitting at an old desk was a graying man who looked up at them as they all came in together.

"Why, Jean, what a surprise! Are you home for the summer?" He stood up and smiled, including the others in his questioning glance.

"*Oui, mon Père.* And these are some of our guests for the summer." Jean introduced everyone.

"Well, I am very honored," Father Thomas said in English. "This library has very few books in English, I'm afraid."

"But that's not why we are here," Eustice said. "We need you to translate something we found at the château."

Father Thomas gave Jean a questioning look. "And what do you need translated?"

Jean reached into his pack and pulled out the book. "This," he said.

"And what is this?" Father Thomas took the book from his hand. His hands caressed the leather binding before opening it. "Why, I haven't seen one of these in years," he said, smiling. Suddenly the smile left his face. *"Mon Dieu,"* he said under his breath.

"Mon Père, what is it?" Jean asked eagerly.

"I can't believe it." Father Thomas sat down at his desk and cleaned his glasses carefully.

"What do you think it could be?" Eustice asked eagerly as he leaned over Father Thomas's shoulder as if to see what so interested the older man.

"May I keep this?" Father Thomas looked at Jean. "It will take me some time to translate it."

"Jean, didn't your father say he needed the book back?" Eustice asked.

"Your father knows you brought this to me?" Father Thomas looked stunned.

"No, he doesn't," Jean said, giving Eustice a quick frown. "That's why I can't leave this here."

Eustice nodded his approval. "That's right. We have to hold onto it or else we will get into trouble."

"It may already be too late for that," Father Thomas said quietly.

"What is it, sir? What does the book mean?" Rachel was worried by the expression on Father Thomas's face.

"It is an old logbook from the war. It once had great value in this community. More value than perhaps anything else you could imagine."

"But why?" Angelica asked.

Father Thomas had forgotten their presence. The book lay open under his hand and Rachel could see his hand tremble.

"It looks to us as if it was a list of some sort," Eustice said, trying to get Father Thomas's attention.

"It is a list. That's exactly what it is. But it is a list that many people thought was destroyed. It will not help anyone here for you to expose this. You must get rid of it."

"But I couldn't! It belongs to my father!"

"Does it, son?"

"But it was at the château!"

"Yes, I can understand that." Father Thomas paused. "So were they," he added simply.

Jean looked annoyed. "We are getting nowhere. Will you tell us about this book or not?"

Father Thomas looked at him kindly. "I am sorry, Jean. This must seem very strange to you that I am so mysterious. I do not mean to be, but I am not dealing with only my secret here. What is contained in this book is of import to many people in this community besides your father. I am surprised that he has kept this for so long. I would have worried had I known."

"Worried about what?"

Father Thomas was looking at the book carefully, shaking his head. "I can't believe that I am seeing this again."

Eustice glanced over at Jean. "This is getting frustrating. Shall we go somewhere else?"

Father Thomas looked at him. "My son, you may go to someone else of course, but you must be careful."

"But if you won't tell us what it is, how will we know how to be careful?"

Father Thomas sighed. "Perhaps you are right. Perhaps you should know."

They heard voices coming toward the library entrance and turned to see two of the men from the café enter. "*Bonjour les enfants! Mon Père*, it is time to join us for cards! You must not hold these children in the library for so long or you will scare them off books forever." They laughed. One of them, a large man with narrow eyes, caught sight of the book on Father Thomas's desk. "Did these young people bring a book to you, mon Père? Isn't that a bit like bringing wine to the vineyard?" He laughed at his own joke but his eyes were wary. Jean snatched the little book off the desk.

"Thank you, *mon Père*, for your advice. Indeed, my father will help us with this assignment I am sure."

Father Thomas's hand caught his arm. "It would be better for you, I know, if you were to leave this here with me."

"Thank you sir, but no. My parents are most strict about others doing work for me," Jean said quickly. Turning to the others, he smiled. "Shall we go?"

The large man stood in the doorway. "That book, Jean. What is it? It has a familiar look to it."

Father Thomas laughed shakily. "Come, come, Pierre! You are showing the nervousness of a bride."

The other man guffawed and slapped his friend on the back. "A bride, Pierre! Would that you were so innocent with the cards, *n'est-ce pas*?"

"We better leave," Rachel said, heading for the door quickly.

"Yes," Jean said, as he followed her. "Come on, Byron, there is nothing more to be found out here."

"Jean!" Father Thomas called after them. Jean turned around and faced him cautiously.

"Oui?"

"You must feel free to come back and ask me more questions any time you feel it is necessary. Will you do that?"

"Of course, *mon Père*. I will let you know of any further questions." Jean waited until he was out in the sunlight before he finished the sentence. "Which will be never," he whispered.

No one said anything at first as they all started their Solexes and followed Jean down the main road back toward the château. Rachel glanced over at Eustice and saw that he, too, was lost in thought. Angelica pulled up next to her. "Slow down a little," Angelica begged.

"Rachel, what do you think this means?" she asked when Eustice and Jean were out of hearing.

"I'm not sure. But I know that it's not good. And I'm not sure we should be involved."

"Perhaps it was a mistake to tell Father Thomas about the book."

"What can we do about it now?"

"We can try to get Eustice off the trail."

"What if Jean wants to pursue it further?" Rachel glanced ahead where Jean was riding by himself. "How hard this must be for him!"

Angelica nodded. "Yes, but this is his decision. We just have to make sure that Eustice doesn't try to influence him to go forward unless he wants to."

Rachel gave a reluctant laugh. "Maybe between the two of us we have a chance."

"Eustice promised. We just hold him to that."

"Angelica, are you scared?"

Angelica looked over at her quickly. "A little."

"Me too."

"Why are you two lagging behind?" Eustice slowed his bike down to join them.

"We wanted to discuss how we are going to get you off this mystery."

"But why? Can't you see we're onto something big?"

"That's just the point, Eustice. This looks a lot bigger than we originally thought."

Eustice pushed his glasses up and continued as if he hadn't heard them. "I mean that guy was flipped out. And he really didn't want those other guys to know what he was looking at. I wonder what is in that list?"

"Eustice, whatever it is, it may cause trouble. Not only for Jean but for his parents," Rachel said softly as she saw that Jean had slowed down for them to catch up.

"What?"

"I said that sometimes I think you like to play deaf," she added angrily.

Jean let them catch up to him and pulled his So-lex next to Rachel's. "Rachel, you are lecturing Byron about something. I can see it. What is this all about?"

"I think Eustice is a stubborn, insensitive lout."

"Thank you, Cousin."

Jean laughed. "Because he is even more curious about the book after Father Thomas's reaction?"

"Yes."

"Well, so am I."

"Way to go, Jean!" Eustice beamed at him. "I mean, this is turning into something pretty big. I can feel it. It would be terrible to stop the investigation now, don't you think?"

"Yes, Byron, but we must be very careful from now on in."

"Of course we'll be careful."

"Let's pull over and go sit under that shady tree over there and discuss this further." Jean pointed to an open field that they were passing. They all pulled their Solexes over to the side of the road and got off, following Jean toward a large tree near the fence. Jean sat down and the others sat facing him. Eustice eagerly pushed his glasses up his nose. "You agree with me that this is worth our pursuing, don't you?"

"I just said that, Byron."

"Then what's the problem? I mean, all we have to do is get a German dictionary and let's figure this out ourselves. I'm sure you have one back at the château."

Jean was quiet for a moment. "I am sure we do, too," he said. "But that's not the point."

"Then what is?"

"I'm not sure. That's why I wanted to think a bit before we get back to the house. First of all, are we going to replace the book?"

Eustice thought for a moment. "It seems to me we have to. Otherwise your parents will know we have found it."

"Yes, but what if they destroy it?"

"Good point." Eustice slapped his knee. "We copy it! And then we return the original to its proper place and work from the copy!"

"That's an idea," Jean said eagerly. "Then no one will know that we have it."

"That's the idea," Eustice said. "What do you think, girls?"

"I think that we're crazy. I'm not kidding, Eustice. I think that this is getting dangerous."

"But we've barely begun!"

"You asked my opinion, you got it."

"And I agree with Angelica," Rachel said softly.

Eustice looked over at Jean. "If you agree with them, Jean, I'll back down. I promised."

"No, Byron. I will make a copy of the book and we will continue this." Jean smiled at him. "But thank you for offering to do what is so against your nature."

Rachel laughed. "I must admit, Eustice, you sure surprised me."

"I will return to the village where the post office has a copy machine. You all go back to the château and wait for me there." Jean rose to his feet. "I will be no more than a half hour."

"Great." Eustice stood up and looked over at the girls. "See? I'm not the only man around here eager to find out the truth."

"Eustice, shut up!"

"Angelica, I didn't force Jean to do anything. You heard me, I offered to stop the whole investigation."

"He's right, Angelica," Rachel added. "And even I am now curious to find out what that book means."

Jean held out his hand for her to take and pulled her to her feet. "Rachel, will you come with me?"

"Hey, I'd love to come too!"

"Byron, this time I'm going to say no to you."

"Eustice, maybe Jean would like to have Rachel's company with him instead of yours."

"Gee, Angelica, you sure do know how to compliment a person."

Angelica put her arm through Eustice's. "Give the guy a chance to spend some time with a pretty girl," she whispered.

"Oh! Now I get it."

"Good boy." Angelica smiled at Rachel. "See you later, Rach. I'll get Mr. Holmes home safely and we'll see you in an hour."

"But Angelica, they said half an hour."

"Eustice, please show a little tact."

Eustice blushed. "Okay, okay. See you when we see you."

They all returned to their Solexes and parted ways, Angelica and Eustice heading back toward the château and Jean, with Rachel, riding back toward the town. As they reached the fringes of the village, Jean pulled over and motioned for Rachel to join him. "I am suddenly wondering how to get by Father Thomas. The post office is next to the library."

"Isn't he playing cards with that man Pierre?"

"Yes, I think so, but we won't know for sure until we are actually in front of the library. And if he is not playing cards, if he is in the library, what shall we do, Rachel?"

"Why don't we walk from here? Leave our bikes in the ditch and peek into the café to make sure Father Thomas is playing his card game. Then you sneak past the library and into the post office and I will stand guard and let you know if anyone is coming."

Jean took her hand and gave it a gentle squeeze. "You are as clever as your cousin, Miss Rachel Smith. And ever so much prettier."

"Hush! We must hurry and get the book copied before Father Thomas returns to work!"

"Oui, ma petite."

Rachel looked down shyly but allowed her fingers to interlace with his. They walked the rest of the way into the village. This time there were no townsmen sitting outside the café.

"This is a good sign," Jean whispered. "They usually play in the back where you cannot see the entrance to either building."

They ran to the door of the post office and slowly entered the dark interior. There wasn't a sound from the main room, but to be sure Rachel tiptoed to the doorway and saw that the postmaster's desk was empty. She waved to Jean who quickly passed her into a smaller room where there was an old copying machine. She followed him and stayed at the door where she could be able to see when Father Thomas returned to the school.

It seemed like hours before Jean had copied the entire book, nearly running out of the necessary change to run the machine. Finally he gave her a quick smile and a thumbs-up before tucking the book and his copy into his shirt. They began to move slowly out of the building toward the front door when they heard voices and Jean tugged her back just before Father Thomas passed by and entered the school.

"What do we do now?" Rachel whispered.

"Hush." Jean's mouth was near her ear. "We wait for a minute and then you sneak out first. I will follow. All we have to do is get by the school door and we will be fine."

"Jean, I'm scared!"

His arm encircled her and he pulled her close. Taking her chin in his hand, he lifted her face up to his and kissed her. "You will be fine," he whispered. "Now go!"

Rachel slowly moved out of the doorway. The entrance to the school was wide open and she could imagine Father Thomas at his desk. She crept quietly by under the windows and waited a moment to try to hear any sounds. A chair scraped against the floor and she could hear Father Thomas moving toward the window. Not bothering to look to see whether he saw her, she ran quickly down the main street and back to where she and Jean had left their Solexes. It seemed forever before she heard Jean running toward her. When he'd joined her and gave her a relieved hug, he whispered, "Success! No one saw us!"

"We hope," Rachel said shakily.

"We hope," he agreed. "Now let's go back to the château, return the book, and let Byron continue his investigation."

They began the trip home, both in good spirits. "I couldn't have done it without you, Rachel," Jean said. "Wouldn't your cousin be proud of your courage!"

"What courage? When I heard Father Thomas coming I thought I would die of terror!"

"You didn't show it, *ma petite*, and for that I will always be grateful."

Rachel laughed. "As I remember, I told you I was terrified."

Jean grinned. "It gave me an excuse to do something I have wanted to do all summer."

"Pull ahead of me," Rachel said. "I hear a car coming."

Jean laughed. "Are you trying to get rid of me, Rachel? It won't work, you know."

Rachel blushed, accelerating so that she went ahead of him. "You are shameless, Jean! Race you back to the château!" She was laughing as she felt her Solex's burst of speed separate them. Let him try to catch her now! She turned her head quickly to make sure that he was behind her and saw the small car moving up behind him. He was grinning at her, pulling his Solex to the side of the road to let the approaching car pass. The sun caught the windshield with a blinding light so that Rachel couldn't see who was driving, but she saw the car swerve and she saw Jean's look of surprise as he felt it hit his Solex. She heard her own scream before she, too, was propelled into the boggy ditch at the side of the road.

Chapter Seven

Rachel!"

"Here, Jean."

"*Mon Dieu*, are you all right?"

"I think so." Rachel got up slowly. "What happened?"

"I'm not sure. That car hit me. I could feel its heat. But why didn't it stop? Did it hit you too?" Jean's face was streaked in mud from the ditch. "I don't understand. Do you think it *meant* to hit us?"

Rachel was wiping the mud off her clothes as best she could while she tried to gather her thoughts. "I don't know, Jean. Did you recognize the car?"

"I didn't see it. Did you?"

"It looked like a blue Fiat. Like your mother's."

"I hardly think that my mother would want to run us down." Jean looked angry. "Besides, my mother's is a Renault, not a Fiat."

"I didn't say that she would." Rachel felt like crying. "I just meant that is was a blue car like hers."

Jean saw the tears in her eyes and came over quickly to hug her hard. "*Chérie*, I am sorry to snap at you. I know you didn't mean to say that *Maman* would hit us. Someone did and that someone had a blue car like hers. That is a good clue, though, is it not?"

"The book, Jean, do you have the book?"

Jean patted his chest. "Both copies are inside my shirt. I am lucky I hid them both away so they weren't damaged by the mud, no?"

"Yes." Rachel smiled at him. "You are very lucky." Suddenly she chuckled.

He frowned at her. "And what is that laugh supposed to mean?"

"It means you look very silly standing there covered with mud, patting your stomach."

Jean laughed, and suddenly both of them sat down and laughed until tears rolled down their cheeks.

"Is this shock, do you think?" Sobbing, Rachel mopped the tears off her face, leaving streaks of dirt behind.

"Could be," gasped Jean, taking her hand and clutching it tightly.

They laughed until they could laugh no more and then they lapsed into silence, each trying to absorb what had just happened.

"*Chérie*, you think that it had to do with the book, don't you?" Jean finally asked.

"Yes. Someone knew that we had it and someone knew we were in town just now. Wouldn't that mean that someone is keeping a pretty close eye on us?"

"Father Thomas?" Jean asked. But he shook his head quickly. "It is not like him to hurt anyone. I cannot believe he would try to hit us."

"What about that big man from the café?" Rachel asked. "What about Pierre?"

"But I got no sense that Pierre had seen what the book was."

"Yes, but he saw how old it was and he was trying to remember where he had seen it before." Rachel slowly got up and went over to see if her Solex was all right. "Well, maybe he remembered."

"If the book is dangerous, it is lucky we copied it and can now return the original to the box in my parents' room." Jean went over to his Solex. "Which I think we should do as quickly as possible."

Much to their relief the Solexes started right away after small muddy splutters. Jean moved his out into the road first and then turned to smile encouragingly at Rachel.

"We're almost home now," he said.

"Which is lucky," she replied feebly. "My knees feel like rubber."

"Just think of how jealous your cousin will be to have missed this." Jean grinned. "I rather think he might almost wish he had been hit too!"

"I think you are getting quite good at predicting Eustice's reactions."

"Byron is pretty easy to read."

Rachel laughed. "He wouldn't be happy to hear you say that."

"I almost can't wait to hear what his next scheme will be, given the nature of our reception just now."

"As long as I don't have to be hit by any more cars I don't care."

"*Pauvre chérie*, we will make sure of that."

They rode the rest of the way back to the château in silence. Rachel didn't even see the lovely country-side that surrounded her, she was lost in thought about how close they had come to being hurt. This was something she would have to discuss with Eustice. He must be made aware of the danger that they were plunging into. Not only Jean, but all of them. The book that now nestled in Jean's shirt was dangerous. Was it worth finding out what the truth was? The car that had just sideswiped them into a ditch was not a joke. And whoever was driving didn't care if he ran down two young kids.

She was relieved to see the old gates of the château looming ahead of them. As they came down the driveway she looked at the viscountess's blue car parked at the door. Could it have been the car that had run them down? She found it hard to believe.

"Nice of you guys to come back so quickly." Eustice gave his watch a quick glance. "That's the longest half hour in the history of time." He looked more carefully at their faces. "Did you stop for a cool wallow in the mud?"

"We were run down by a car a few kilometers from town."

"What?"

"That's right, Byron. If there hadn't been a ditch full of muddy water you might not have seen us again."

Angelica joined them. Disregarding their disheveled appearance she asked, "You guys had fun?"

"Being hit by a car is always a thrill, Angelica."

"What?"

"The book, man, what happened to the book?" Eustice asked impatiently.

"Don't worry, Byron. Thank you for your flattering concern for both me and your cousin."

"I didn't mean it like that, Jean. I can see you both are all right, thank heaven. But the book, did you save that?"

"I saved both the original and the copy."

"Great! Now we can return the original and continue the investigation. Your father has been in his study ever since we got back. I have a feeling that we'd better get the book back where it belongs before the day is out.''

"And then we have to find a German dictionary," Angelica said.

"I was thinking about that," Jean said. "I was thinking that Hans could tell us what it meant."

"But Hans is German!"

"Of course he is, that's why he's the perfect person to ask."

"But Jean—"

Jean interrupted him. "Byron, the war ended over forty years ago. Hans can help us. This is history, Eustice. To exclude Hans is to accuse him of something he has had no involvement in. Don't you think it would make it more interesting to bring in the others from Château Menat?"

"I think you're right," Angelica said. "It's a great idea to include Hans and the others. I would be very interested to hear what Hans has to say about it. Besides," she added wickedly, "that means you can get more information from Sabine, Eustice!"

"Then we will go with the copy to the Château Menat tomorrow," Jean said. "Sabine will indeed be very useful because her parents were also here during the Occupation years."

Eustice was silent for a moment then he spoke up. "You're right, of course, and I should have seen it too. This book could be something for all of us to learn from."

"I think you are all crazy," Rachel said hotly. "I think that we will be involving all those nice kids in something that seems too dangerous for us. Too dangerous even for your parents, Jean! You heard Father Thomas! He said that your father never should have kept the book. He said that the book should have been destroyed. You heard him!"

"Yes, Rachel, I heard him. But I think that the more of us that know about this, the better. Then we can all help each other. Who knows how many of those bad guys there are?"

Eustice nodded. "I think he's right, Rach."

"So do I," Angelica agreed.

"Have it your way," Rachel said. "I'm going upstairs to bathe and change. I don't care what you do. I don't even care if you all get killed. I'm just too tired and frightened to argue."

"Atta girl!"

"Shut up, Eustice!" Rachel felt tears in her eyes.

Angelica came over and put an arm around her. "Let's go upstairs and get you cleaned up. Jean will return the book and then no one will even know we have it any more."

"Only the person who tried to kill us."

"Maybe it was an accident. Maybe they didn't mean to hit you."

"That would be a fair assumption, Eustice, only they kept right on going. Have you ever heard of someone hitting two kids and continuing on his merry way?"

Jean went over to Rachel and gave her a hug. "You are a courageous girl, Rachel Smith, and I think we should listen carefully to your advice. But don't you agree that we must continue to pursue this? After all, the person who tried to kill us today will not know that we have given up the search. So if that person is going to continue to try to kill us, we should be just as quickly trying to find out why he or she wants us dead, *n'est-ce pas*?"

"I guess so," Rachel said reluctantly. "But now I am only going to think about getting these filthy clothes off."

"I'm proud of you," Eustice said.

"Byron is right," Jean said softly. "Now go and take your bath. We will see you later."

Rachel and Angelica walked into the house and headed toward their room. They ran into the viscountess coming out of the kitchen. Noticing Rachel's muddy face and clothes, she stopped.

"Goodness *mon enfant*, what has happened to you?"

"I fell off my Solex, Madame. It was very silly and clumsy of me."

"But are you all right?" The viscountess looked so genuinely concerned that Rachel felt even more confident that this was not the driver of the car that had hit them.

"I think so. After a hot bath I know I will be just fine, thank you." Rachel gave her a wan smile.

"You must not go so fast on these country roads, you are not used to them. I will make sure that Jean is more careful. And where is Jean?"

"I think he went upstairs," Angelica said quickly. "The last time I saw him he was headed in that direction."

The viscountess, with one final worried glance at Rachel, left them and headed toward Jean's room. Angelica turned back to Rachel and said, "You go on up and start your bath. I'm just going to warn Jean to stay away from his room until his mother has left. It might make her suspicious for her to see him as muddy as you!"

Rachel went into her room and peeled off the now dry and caked clothes. Going into the bathroom, she started the water and sat watching it flow into the tub issuing great clouds of comforting steam. Never in her life had she been so homesick as she was at that moment. When the bath was full, she shut off the water and slowly sank into the warm depths. Feeling the soothing water and thinking of her home in Massachusetts started the tears all over again. Angelica, coming to check up on her, heard her quiet sobs.

"Rach, are you all right in there?"

"Yes, I think so."

Angelica peered in. "You want some company?"

"I'll be okay. I think that I'm having another delayed reaction. But, Angelica, I'm so scared! That driver wasn't kidding."

Angelica came in and sat. "Look, Rachel, I'll talk to Eustice again, but Jean has a point about the person who hit you. If he thinks we have the book now, how will he know that we've returned it? We *have* to see this through now, otherwise we'll be in danger the whole summer."

"I want to go home."

"What? And leave that handsome Jean who seems crazy about you? Rachel, sometimes I think you're crazy." Angelica smiled.

Rachel gave a shaky laugh. "He is kind of handsome, isn't he?"

"Handsome isn't the right word, kid. Devastating is more like it."

Rachel gave Angelica a wan smile. "I feel better now, Angelica. Thank you."

"Don't be silly, Rach. If I had just been swiped by a car I would expect you to do the same for me." Angelica grinned down at her. "Now I think that I can leave you to bathe in privacy!" She slipped out and left Rachel smiling to herself.

Eustice met her in the hallway. "How is she?" he asked.

"Understandably flipped out."

Eustice nodded. "Even Jean is flipped out. Did you see his mother?"

"She was looking for him but I thought I got her off the trail by sending her to his room."

"You did. She found me instead." Eustice shook his head. "She's a little skittery about something."

"Maybe she knows that we took the book."

He nodded. "Maybe. There's no way for us to find out, though, without spilling the beans. We'll have to listen as hard as we can for clues."

"What about the viscount?"

"As far as I know, he's been in the study all day."

"Hush!" Angelica said. "Do you hear that?"

"What?"

"A car coming down the driveway." Angelica flew to the window that overlooked the long drive. "It *is* a car! Oh, Eustice, I'm afraid!"

"Angelica, calm down. It could be anybody."

Angelica glanced out the window, trying to stay out of sight of the people below. "It's someone I've never seen before," she whispered.

Eustice peered over her shoulder. "It looks like the farmer we passed when we first arrived. I bet he's just a neighbor dropping by."

"There's the viscount!"

Sure enough, the viscount came slowly down the front stone steps, leaning heavily on his cane. Angelica could see him speaking with the farmer.

"What is he saying?"

"Eustice, I can't hear and I can't speak French. How am I supposed to know what he is saying?"

The two men stood for quite a while speaking in low tones. After a few minutes, the viscountess came down the steps to join them, hooking her arm through the viscount's as if to give him some support.

"They don't look very pleased," Eustice whispered.

"She looks scared, doesn't she, Eustice?"

"Maybe. Let's not jump to conclusions, though."

After what seemed to be a long time, the farmer got back into his old truck and drove slowly away. The viscount and viscountess watched him go and then turned back toward the house. Suddenly the viscount looked up at the window and Angelica could tell that he had seen them.

"Oh, no. What are we going to do now?" Angelica asked.

"Don't be silly," Eustice said sternly. "We have every right to look out the window." He squeezed her arm. "Angelica, we've got to keep our cool, otherwise we're lost."

"He's right, Angelica." Jean stood behind them, his dark eyes serious. "We must be very discreet and calm."

Eustice smiled at him. "Jean, you're a good man."

Jean smiled. "A good clean man, thank heaven. Now I have to figure out how to wash my filthy clothes."

"Rachel and I can do that here," Angelica said. "When will you return the book to the box?"

Jean smiled. "It has already been done. I heard my parents go downstairs and slipped it into the box then. So now we are all set to pursue our investigation without worrying about their figuring out we have seen the book."

"If they haven't figured it out already," Eustice said. "They looked pretty serious talking with the farmer who was just here."

Jean shook his head. "That was only Maurice. He owns the land next to ours and he comes over often to discuss using some of our land to graze his sheep."

Eustice shook his head, remembering the viscount's sharp look that had caught him at the window with Angelica. "All I can say is that I hope you're right."

Chapter Eight

The next day the four started off early for the Château Menat. They had gone no farther than a few kilometers when Jean waved that he was pulling over to the side of the road. The others joined him and when he turned off his Solex they did the same.

"What's the problem, Jean?" Eustice asked.

"Nothing much, Bryon. I just wanted to let you know that my mother suspects something."

"What?"

"Last night she came into my room and asked me if I had been disturbing the books in the study."

"What did you say?"

"I said that I had been looking for a book that you had asked me about concerning the history of France." Jean smiled. "I know that my father has such a book and I said that you wanted to read it. When we get back she will probably give it to you."

"And I'm supposed to look like the happy scholar, is that it?"

"That's right."

"Got it. But was she happy with your explanation?"

"Not totally, but she seemed relieved." Jean looked serious. "I think that we must try to move quickly on finding out what the book means."

"Then let's get going." Eustice started up his Solex.

Rachel watched the two boys as she got her machine started and began to move down the road after them. She had woken up stiff that morning but feeling better about the situation. Seeing that Jean was calm and knowing that he had returned the book without too much ado had lessened her terror about the viscount and viscountess being angry. Today, knowing that they were going to get the book translated and were going to involve the kids from Château Menat also made her feel a bit more secure. Safety in numbers was what Eustice had said. She saw that Angelica looked at her with a concerned expression and she smiled to reassure her friend.

Earlier that morning Angelica had woken her up, shaking her gently.

"Hey, Rach, you're crying."

Indeed, Rachel had been crying in her sleep but she couldn't remember the dream that had caused it except the feeling that there had been a great deal of confusion and she had seen Jean's face covered in mud and blood. She shuddered, accelerating the engine of her Solex. Soon they would show the book to Hans and would then know what they were dealing with. If only she could get rid of this sick sense she had that something was going to go terribly wrong.

"*Chérie*, you have barely said a word all day. Are you all right?" Rachel hadn't noticed Jean slowing down to pull his bike next to hers. She met his concerned look with a smile.

"Yes, Jean, I'm okay."

"You must not worry, Rachel. We will know what we have in just a little while."

"I know."

His eyes warmed as they looked at her. "And I can't wait to see that look of worry leave your lovely face," he whispered.

"I just hope that we don't find out anything that will hurt you, Jean."

His smile tightened. "So do I."

They reached the Château Menat. "Now we can find out!" Rachel said. "At last."

"There they are at the tennis court!" Eustice waved at Sabine who had lifted her racket to signal them over.

"Good. We can speak privately there," Jean said.

Hans, Jack and Manuel were rallying on the court and Jack shouted to Angelica to join them in doubles. Angelica shook her head and pointed at Jean and Sabine who were already engaged in conversation. The three boys stopped playing and sauntered off the court. Rachel overheard Sabine say, "Of course you must ask him, Jean. I am sure he would know." Turning to Rachel she gave an excited smile. "Isn't this some adventure you have found?"

"Maybe too much of one." Rachel laughed.

"Too much of what?" Jack asked, as he and the others joined them.

Eustice began, "Well, it seems as if we have gotten ourselves into a bit of a bind. You, Hans, could do us a tremendous service by giving us a translation of some material that seems to date back to World War II and the occupation of France by the German army. Do you mind our asking? I mean it seems to me that this all took place a long time ago, but I sure wouldn't want you to feel awkward about it."

"About what?" Hans asked carefully.

Jean reached into his pack and pulled out his copy of the book. "This," he said.

Hans took the copy out of his hands and started to sift slowly through the pages. "This looks like a journal," he said.

"That's what we've been able to figure out," Eustice said. "But we also know that there seems to be some mystery in it still. That's why we thought you were the person to ask about it."

"It seems this is a list of people who worked for the German army during the war," he said.

"Of course," Eustice whispered, looking over at Jean. "That's just what it is. A list of people in this community who cooperated with the Germans. And that's why someone would want to get rid of it!"

Hans looked up at him. "Yes, I would imagine that there would be a great many people who would be upset to know that this still existed."

"Could you translate it for us, Hans?" Jean asked.

"Yes, if you want me to."

"Are you sure you won't mind?" Rachel asked gently.

"Not at all." Hans smiled at her. "For me, the war was an ugly period in our history that took place a long time ago."

"If the names in that book are the French men and women who collaborated with the Germans," Eustice looked over at Jean, "we could be in big trouble."

Sabine broke into the conversation. "Yes, but look at us now, all from different countries, some that were divided then. For us the war can be something to learn from, no?"

"Yes," Hans said. "Although I think it will never be a wound that will heal entirely."

"Hans, you cannot take it personally," Rachel said. "We are a new generation. Now we have to deal with the nuclear age."

"Maybe the holocaust shows us that we are all capable of horrible things. And our generation must take the responsibility that this doesn't happen again."

"Now that we all have the power to blow up the world," Jack agreed.

Eustice laughed. "Will you listen to this? I wish they let kids have a say in politics. We'd tell them something, wouldn't we, Hans?"

"I could tell them that as evil as the Nazis were, there are good people in Germany."

"And I'd tell them that as bossy and pushy as we Americans seem to be, we can sometimes cope with a touch of humility."

"You can?"

"Shut up, Angelica, you're ruining my speech."

"And I would say that as beautiful a country as Spain is, we still have a long way to go to make the many different Spaniards content with their form of government," Manuel added.

"And I would say that France is just as lovely as everyone says it is," Sabine said, as the others all burst out laughing.

"I think she has a point," Eustice said.

"You would," Angelica teased.

"So do I," Hans agreed.

"Does this mean that we can all agree to try to find out why people are out to kill us?" Rachel asked.

"I think so," Hans said. "I will go over this tonight and we will come over tomorrow and discuss it further. But what do you mean that someone is trying to kill you?"

Jean told him about the day before.

"I can see it." Hans nodded. "In my country, as well, the war brings out dangerous emotions. You must be careful, all of you. If they came after you once, they will come again."

"That's why we came to you, Hans."

On the way home from the Château Menat, Eustice was the first to speak. "I think that Hans was genuinely willing to give us a hand in this, don't you, Jean?"

"Yes. I think we were smart to bring them into this mystery."

"Hey, Jean, why has it taken you so long to confront your father about his part in the war?"

"We've already discussed this," Jean said shortly.

"I didn't mean to pry, man."

"I know, Byron."

Rachel saw Jean's face tighten as he accelerated his Solex to move out ahead of them. Poor Jean, how hard this was on him! Rachel knew that part of his reluctance had to do with Madame but she sensed that there was something more. She remembered her conversation with Jean when they were searching for the book in the master suite. He had been born late in the viscount's life and well into their marriage. It must be hard to be the only child of such a proud old father who so clearly loved his young beautiful wife. Rachel thought of her own parents in Massachusetts. How different they were! Her father and mother were so informal compared to the viscount and viscountess. It was as if Jean believed the viscount didn't want his son to interfere with his life. Yet Rachel found it hard to believe that the viscount didn't love Jean. Looking at him riding his Solex, his features so like his father's, Rachel couldn't and wouldn't believe that this wasn't a son to be proud of. Whatever they discovered in this crazy mystery that they were on to, it would be better for Jean. She truly believed it now. No matter what it was, it would take some of the mystery away from his father and bring him closer to Jean.

"Penny for your thoughts, Rach?" Angelica pulled her Solex next to Rachel's.

"I'm just thinking how courageous Jean is."

"Yes, that's for sure. He could be in deep trouble if the viscount and viscountess find out about our taking the book before we've unraveled the mystery."

"I hope that Hans works quickly."

"Sabine was as anxious as Eustice; she'll stay on top of this until we find an answer."

"It was kind of Hans not to get upset about the war."

"Why should he? He wasn't born yet. His parents were probably not even born yet."

"You know, I hope we resolve this whole mess soon so that we can all just settle down and enjoy each other." Rachel smiled at Angelica. "I really like the kids from Château Menat and I think we could just have fun riding around the countryside learning a little French."

Angelica nodded. "I'll say. Given the speed with which this adventure has progressed so far, I am pretty sure there will be some kind of resolution soon. My only worry is that it won't be a very quiet one."

"Well, here we are." Rachel turned her Solex into the gate of the château.

"And there are the boys waiting patiently for us." Angelica waved as they passed Eustice and Jean by the gate. "Last one home is a rotten *oeuf*!"

Eustice was the first to notice the car in the driveway next to the viscount's. "Hey, Jean, who do you think that is?"

"*Mon Dieu*, I think that is the car of Father Thomas."

"What could he be doing here?" Eustice asked. "You don't think that he has come about the book, do you?"

Jean turned to Rachel and Angelica. "I think it best if we split up here and meet later. I am sure that if it is Father Thomas my father will want to speak to me, alone."

"Oh, Jean, will you be all right?" Rachel asked.

He smiled at her. "I will be fine. I would like to find out though why Father Thomas came to my parents without telling me."

"Let me go with you, Jean. Your folks won't be nearly as tough if I'm with you," Eustice suggested.

"Perhaps, but I think you should take the girls up the back stairs. I will try to come by before dinner and let you know what happened. But you will see me there at any rate. Now hurry!"

He gestured for Rachel and Angelica to lead the way into the back of the house. Eustice followed them reluctantly. When he appeared at the door to their room his look of concern had changed to a full scowl.

"You look like the devil," Angelica said cheerfully.

"I'm worried about Jean. I think I should be with him."

"Eustice, he knows his parents better than you do. If he thought it would be best to face them alone, I'd trust him."

"Angelica's right," Rachel agreed.

"I don't think so. I'm going to see what's going on."

"Eustice, you can't. Jean said not to!"

"Rachel, he didn't say that I couldn't listen, only that I couldn't be there. I'm just going to walk into the main part of the house and up the stairs, and maybe I'll hear something."

"If you go, I go," Rachel said stubbornly.

"Now, Rach—"

"And if Rachel goes, I go."

"Angelica!"

Angelica grinned over at Rachel. "Now we've got him."

"Let's go." Rachel smiled.

"Okay, but you do as I say and stay *behind* me. Is that clear?"

"Perfectly," Angelica said.

They moved quickly down the back stairs and past the kitchen door where they heard Danielle beginning preparations for dinner. In the evenings the main part of the house had a totally different feel from the back quarters where their rooms were. The formality and age of the rooms and of the furniture lent the house a cold feeling, very unlike the nice, comfortable, but somewhat shabby rear section of the château.

"Every time I come into this part of the house I can see why Jean likes to come see us rather than have us come see him."

"I suppose you'd get used to this," Rachel said, looking at the walls and walls of enormous paintings of very serious ancestors.

"Hush! I hear voices." Rachel pulled Angelica with her behind a large screen that separated the entrance to the foyer from the hallway that led to the living room, library and ballroom. Eustice moved across the hall to a large potted plant and stooped down out of sight. They heard the viscount moving slowly and painfully down the stairs but it was the viscountess's voice that arrested them.

"You were very kind to come, *mon Père*. I am sure that Jean must have an explanation. Perhaps it was a project he is working on for school."

"*Mais non*, Madame, I am sure of what I saw."

"That is absolutely impossible. I once knew of such a book, *mon Père*, but it was destroyed many years ago."

"I believe you, Madame, of course." Father Thomas shrugged. "But I know what I saw. And I saw the record book. Your son had it. And, if you will forgive me, Madame, I think that he will be in danger until it has been found."

Jean looked flushed and angry. "Really, *Maman*! I cannot believe it could be the book Father Thomas speaks of. It is impossible!"

"Where did you find it, son?" the viscount asked.

"In the library as I looked for the book Eustice wanted to see on the war. It was next to that."

"And you say you lost it?"

Rachel could see that Father Thomas was watching Jean carefully. Jean looked defiantly right into his eyes. "I thought it might be important after showing it to you. But yesterday, when Rachel and I were sideswiped by a car, I fell into a ditch of mud, and the book was destroyed."

"Jean, you were hit by a car?" Madame's face was ashen. "You said nothing about this!"

"I said nothing, *Maman*, because I was ashamed that I had taken something so valuable from your study to ask Father Thomas about. And when it was destroyed by the mud, I thought it best to say nothing." Jean looked at his father who was frowning in concern. "I am sorry for all this, Papa. Do you think it could have been the book of which you speak?"

"But Roland, he was hit by a car! What car? And who was driving?"

"It was blue. I saw no one, *Maman*."

"And the book was destroyed? Are you sure?" Father Thomas didn't sound convinced. The viscount drew himself up. "This is all we have to say at this time. My son has had his say and I believe him totally. I think he has learned his lesson and the book, if it was the logbook, has been destroyed. No one needs to worry about this matter any further."

"Oh I doubt that, viscount. I doubt that very much."

"Good night, *mon Père*. Thank you for coming all this way to warn us." The viscountess put one arm through her husband's and drew Jean close with the other. "I think that now we will take these matters into our own hands."

"And tell Pierre that, either way, the book no longer exists."

"Pierre?" Father Thomas looked surprised. "What has Pierre to do with this?" He cleared his throat and his eyes shifted back and forth between the viscount and viscountess.

"A silly question to ask in front of me, Thomas." The viscount looked down at his wife. "If we find out any further information we will let you know." He started to head toward the large living room. "Good night, Thomas."

"Good night, Monsieur, Madame. And good night, Jean." Father Thomas gave a slight bow and moved toward the door. As he opened it, he paused and turned back again to look at them. "As I have said, I do think you should be very careful until you have proof that the book was truly destroyed."

"Look in the ditch where the car ran Rachel and me down and you will find it!" Jean said hotly.

"I will probably have to," Father Thomas said, opening the door and quietly walking out.

They could hear his car start up and move down the driveway.

The viscount cleared his throat. "I need a drink," he said to his wife. Together they moved into the great living room.

Jean paused as if deciding whether or not to join them. Eustice peered out from behind the potted plant.

"Psst!"

"What are you doing here? I thought I told you that everything would be all right!" Jean said angrily.

Rachel moved out from behind the screen. "So you did."

"My parents will have a fit if they find you three here. You must go back to your rooms!" His voice was stern but his eyes pleaded with Rachel.

"Aren't you going to tell them that the book is safe? And that we have another copy?"

"All in good time, Byron."

"You mean you don't trust them with our secret?"

"Jean, come here!" the viscount called from the living room.

Jean shook his head. "You were not there, Byron, but I could tell that they were frightened by Father Thomas."

"Who wouldn't be?"

"Don't you see?" Jean's eyes were bright with feeling. "I have to know more before I let them in on our secret."

"Jean!"

Jean pushed Eustice toward the girls. "Now go! I'll meet you after dinner and we can plan everything."

Chapter Nine

I don't like this one bit.'' Eustice flopped down on one of the beds and frowned as he put his chin in his hands.

"None of us are exactly crazy about this situation," Angelica said. "Have you forgotten it was your idea?"

"No. Well, this time I've learned. No more mysteries for me!"

Eustice looked at his watch. "Listen, it's almost time for dinner. Let's see how Jean is taking it and we'll discuss this later."

The next half hour went very slowly. They knew that they couldn't go down too early for dinner or they would appear too anxious, so the three of them played a bad-tempered game of gin rummy. When Eustice lost for the third time he threw down his cards. "I don't care if we are early, let's go."

"Right." Both Angelica and Rachel leaped off the bed after him.

They went downstairs and into the kitchen where Danielle, smiling cheerfully, told then that dinner would be in another ten minutes.

"Shall we go sit in the dining room?" Rachel asked.

"Too early. Let's just walk around the house. By that time it'll be time to join the family."

"Good idea, Byron." Angelica headed out the back door.

"Don't call me that!" Eustice followed her.

The three of them walked slowly through the old formal gardens at the back of the château. Although sadly in need of some good pruning and cutting there were still signs of the original topiary. Two elephants stood guard at one corner. The shapes were still obvious although the wire mesh that formed the animals was clearly visible through the old bush structure.

"I think it's kind of cool the way those bushes are trimmed," Angelica said.

"Be quiet. I hear something!" Rachel grabbed her arm. "Over there, it's coming from over there."

They all stopped and listened. At first there was no sound except the distant mooing of the cows being milked. Angelica was just about to admonish Rachel for scaring them when the sound came again. Rachel clutched her hand. "There!" she whispered.

They listened to the sound of footsteps crunching on the gravel of the garden walk. Crouched behind the bushes, it was hard to see, but as they waited they saw a shadowy form move along the side of the house.

"Someone is trying to get into the house!" Eustice said tensely. He pushed his glasses up his nose trying to see more clearly.

"Not one, Eustice, *three*." Angelica pointed. "Look."

Behind the first shadowy figure slipped a second and then a third. The lights in the dining room were on and the children could see the viscount and viscountess enter the room and sit down for dinner. Jean pushed in his mother's chair for her and stood behind his own as if waiting for Eustice and the others to enter. Under the bright lights of the chandelier the young people watched the three figures enter the dining room and surround the little family.

"Oh boy, what are we going to do now?" Eustice's voice was a mere squeak.

"They even have Danielle!" Angelica whispered as they saw Danielle innocently push open the pantry door and enter with the first course.

"Is that the big man from yesterday? Is that Pierre?" Angelica pointed to the large man whose back was against the glass doors of the dining room.

"Who else could it be?" Rachel asked.

"We have to get help. And fast," Eustice said.

"But they'll hear us if we start our Solexes! And in a car they will catch us right away."

"Not if we pedal down the drive and then start the engines out of their hearing."

"But one of us has to stay here and witness this! What if they hurt the family?"

"You're right, Cousin. You will have to stay, but stay out of sight, do you hear me? No matter what happens, Rachel, stay out of their sight!" Eustice clutched her arm firmly and made her meet his eyes. "I won't have you hurt. Something very terrible is going on here and you must not get involved. Even if—"

"If what?" Rachel whispered.

"If anything happens," Eustice said firmly.

"Look, they're even searching our rooms!" Angelica cried out.

They could see the lights to their rooms being turned on and the figure of a man moving through each of the servants' quarters turning lights on and off as he went.

"They are looking for us," Eustice said. "We have to move, and quickly!"

"Where do we go?"

"We have to go to the Château Menat and alert the others. We need all the help we can get." Eustice looked over at Angelica. "You go into town and see if you can find a police officer. Bring him too."

"But I can't speak French!"

"Then let Rachel go."

"No!" Rachel cried. "I want to stay here, if something happens I want to help Jean!" She turned to Angelica. "Go on, you know how to say help in French. You can do it, Angelica."

"Mon Dieu."

"That's right! Keep that French coming. Now let's get out of here before they do anything."

Rachel shivered as Eustice and Angelica slipped out of her sight and moved quietly around the house toward where they had parked their Solexes. Three minutes later, Eustice was back. "There's someone guarding the car and our Solexes! You have to create a diversion, Rachel."

"What'll I do?"

"Come with me and make a noise to get their attention. While they look for you, Angelica and I will get out of here." He squeezed her hand. "We have to do this, Rach. Otherwise they might hurt Jean and his family."

"Right." Rachel gathered her courage and followed him around the house. Sure enough, there was a man standing in front of the shed that held their Solexes. Eustice moved away from her and after waiting for him to get out of range, Rachel gritted her teeth, drew a deep breath and then stood up.

"Excuse me, but were you invited for dinner?" she asked the surprised-looking man in front of the shed.

"Viens ici!" he said, moving toward her and gesturing for her to come to him.

"What did you say?" She backed away a little and he moved toward her.

"Viens ici!" he repeated and when she turned from him he shouted, "Pierre! Pierre, *ici!*"

Rachel began to run and the man took off after her. She ran behind the house toward the safety of the gardens. She could hear the man behind her gasping for breath, and she increased her speed. She had never been so scared in her life but felt a sudden surge of energy as she saw the garden up ahead. Any second now she would be out of sight and hard to find. She almost sobbed with joy as she speeded past the topiary elephants.

Turning a corner she found herself in the arms of a large, strong man. Her scream was muffled by a fat unclean hand. He lifted her off her feet and carried her back to the house, ignoring her kicks and attempts at biting the fingers that tightened around her face.

He carried her into the dining room and put her gently down on a chair. Her mouth stung from the force of his hand and she rubbed it angrily as she met the gaze of her captor. Indeed it was the same man who had come to see Father Thomas in the school library. Pierre.

"Do you own a blue car?" she asked him.

"Rachel, hush!" Jean's anxious face caught her attention.

"We are not here to hurt you. Any of you. We want the book."

"You mean the book that was destroyed?" Jean asked.

"You must stop this, Jean, you do not know anything about this book and the history it contains. You have nothing to forget, boy. And what is in that book is something to forget. Monsieur le Vicomte, tell your son. Tell him what he was holding in his hand and showing to Father Thomas. Tell him what it meant and why I am here."

"The book has been destroyed. You heard my son. You may go home, Pierre."

"We believed you once, Monsieur le Vicomte. Before you became a Nazi-lover. Now we must see the evidence." Pierre looked at the other three men who were with him. "Perhaps when we see that it has truly been destroyed, we will leave and forget all about this. But if we don't, someone will be hurt." He drew a long knife out of a sheath attached to his belt. "Tell him, Monsieur," he insisted.

"How dare you speak like that to my father!" Jean said hotly.

"Hush, son. I will say nothing. These things are to be forgotten. They concern ghosts from forty years ago!"

"They concern us, Monsieur. We are not ghosts."

"Roland, don't make them angry." The viscountess turned to Pierre. "He doesn't know about the book, it was I. My husband did not know until recently that I saved it all these years. I hid it away in the carriage house after they left, before the Americans came. I hid it away in case I needed proof—"

"Michelle!" The viscount tried to get up and go over to her but Pierre pushed him back down into his seat.

"Go on, Madame," he said.

"I hid it away because Roland wouldn't talk of what happened here. The book was evidence. Evidence he wanted to forget," she said with an agonized look at her husband. "And they dare call you a Nazi-lover," she said angrily.

"Michelle, you were a young girl, you know nothing about this! Please, *mignonne*, say nothing more!"

"When they shot you, when they put you up against the wall of your own home and shot you, Roland, you think I could forget?" The viscountess shook her head. "Oh, I know about all of it. And I know of your courage. And I know," she whispered, "that if I didn't save that record there would be no evidence of your sacrifice."

"Papa!" Jean cried.

"I didn't care, Michelle! You must understand. I don't care now." The viscount cast a quick look at Jean. "I have never felt that anyone could explain the horror of that time. None of it matters except to make our children forget such sorrow ever existed."

"And the book?" Pierre asked. "Where is the book?"

"My son says it was destroyed. I believe him."

"Oh, Papa." Jean sobbed. "I don't understand any of this!"

"Jean, I never wanted you to understand. What father would want such horrors to be known to his children?"

"The book still exists," Jean whispered. "It is in the library where *Maman* left it."

"Jean! No!" The viscountess put her hand on her mouth.

"Get it, son," the viscount commanded. "There is no going back. We now must face it all over again."

Jean ran out of the room and came back a few minutes later holding the book in his hand. Pierre grabbed it from him and looked at it carefully. He nodded. "This is it."

"And now what do you plan to do to us, Pierre? Shoot us?" The viscount looked at him disdainfully.

"You think that you were such a hero, eh? You housed the Germans for five years and you think that you were a hero. Well, this book should set things straight, right Monsieur le Vicomte d'Ambert? Or will it prove you the hero your wife says you were? I wonder."

"Read the book, Pierre. You will see that there were others who had to collaborate with the Germans besides yourself," the viscount said quietly. "And then there were those who made the Germans *think* they were collaborating."

"Like you, Roland," the viscountess said tenderly. "Like you."

"Papa. Oh, Papa," Jean whispered.

Pierre slapped the viscount so hard that his chair fell over and he crashed to the floor. Jean screamed and flew at Pierre, kicking and scratching him as Pierre tried to peel him off.

"Stop him or I will hurt him!" Pierre cried as his friends tried to pull Jean away.

"Jean, no!" Both Rachel and the viscountess screamed at the same time.

The book fell to the floor and the viscountess flew over, picked it up and held it over her head. "Stop this at once!"

"Give me the book." One of the men moved toward the viscountess who quickly tossed it to Rachel. As one of the others caught Rachel's arm, she threw it back to the viscountess. Pierre pulled out his knife and pulled Jean tightly to him. "One more move and the boy will suffer."

Everyone in the room froze. "Leave my son, please," the viscount said as he struggled to get to his feet.

"Don't give him the book, *Maman*!" Jean said stubbornly, but the viscountess had already handed the book back to one of the men.

"And what are you going to do with this now that you have it?" she asked.

"We will destroy it in our own fashion, Madame," Pierre said. Turning to his friends, he waved them out of the room. "I think we can go now before anyone else loses control, eh?"

"What if we tell the police, what then?" Jean asked him hotly. "Are you planning to leave town, Pierre?"

Pierre gave a short laugh. "Telling the police will do nothing. Don't you understand, boy? This book reveals secrets from a time where there was no law. I don't even think that our police will wish this book to exist."

"So you will destroy it?"

Pierre nodded. "Eventually."

"Then why did you care that we had it?"

"The wrong hands, boy." Pierre grinned at him, showing dark, rotted teeth.

"It is quite clear, Pierre, that you have something quite horrible to hide," Jean said.

"Oh, Jean, please!" his mother cried out.

"Tell him, Madame. Tell him what it was like to live here then. Or are you too proud, like your husband?"

The viscount had by now risen to his feet. "You have the book, Pierre, so now you may leave. We have nothing more to say."

Pierre nodded. "Yes." He bowed mockingly at them all. "I am sorry that we cannot stay to dinner," he said, "but my friends are probably anxious to get back to the café where there are others waiting."

"You will be hearing from us again," the viscount said angrily.

Pierre laughed. "Will I, Monsieur le Vicomte? Will I indeed?" He laughed again and shook his head. "I think that your wife will not allow that. Am I right, Madame?"

"Get out," she whispered, tightly holding on to her son.

"You heard her," Jean said quietly. "Get out and never come back!"

Chapter Ten

W here is everybody?"

Eustice came bursting into the dining room clutching Sabine by the hand. She said breathlessly, "My parents are coming in the car but we came the fastest way possible. Where is Pierre?"

"They are all gone," Jean said quietly.

"But they can't be!" Eustice looked so disappointed that Rachel stifled a nervous chuckle. Jack, Manuel and Hans dashed in. Hans was brandishing a cricket mallet.

"What's that for?" Jean asked.

"Eustice told us you were in danger." Hans looked embarrassed as he put the mallet down. "Obviously he was mistaken."

"And we left our dinner for nothing," Manuel said plaintively.

"Wait a minute, guys, this was serious! Tell them, Jean." Eustice pushed his glasses up his nose. "There were three of them. I swear! Tell them, Jean!"

"There were three of them," Jean said.

"And it was serious," Rachel continued, with a shudder.

"But we gave them what they wanted and they left." Jean looked over at his parents.

"Yes, children, everything is over now." The viscount stood up slowly. "And so I must see if Danielle can feed all of us since you were so good to come."

"Papa, this won't do!" Jean cried.

"What are you talking about?" The viscount frowned.

"Everything!"

The viscount looked over at his wife and then back at the young people who were now facing him with curious expressions on their faces.

"Perhaps another time, son. This does not involve you."

Jean stood up and defiantly faced his father. "Yes, Papa, it does involve all of us. See? My friends went to get help and Sabine brought help. They know of the book because I made a copy and Hans has been translating it for us."

"You made a copy?" The viscountess gasped. "How long have you known about this?"

"Since you brought it in from the carriage house, *Maman*. Eustice saw you and we began to investigate then. I didn't say anything in front of Pierre for obvious reasons. But a copy exists and all of us know about it. So don't you think we should understand what it means?"

"I would like the copy, son."

"Only if you tell us what all this has been about."

"I hear a car." The viscountess got up and went out of the room. Within seconds she had returned with the count and countess de Menat, who greeted the viscount warmly.

"We seem to have had an incident," the viscount said, attempting a smile.

The count de Menat nodded his head. "Yes, Sabine showed us the copy of the logbook, Roland. It gave us quite a start to see that again."

"Won't you explain it to us?" Sabine went over to her father and touched his sleeve. "Don't you think we deserve to know what it means?"

The count looked over at the viscount. "This is your story, Roland."

"And my wife's," the viscount said, exchanging an affectionate look with the viscountess.

"You see, I saved the book," the viscountess explained. "Even Roland wanted it destroyed."

"Why did you save it, Michelle?" the countess de Menat asked gently.

"And what *is* it?" Eustice interrupted.

The viscountess began, "It is a book that was kept by my husband during the war when the Germans occupied this village and made this house their headquarters." She paused.

"Go on, *Maman*, what do all the names mean?"

The viscountess gave herself a little shake as if to gather her thoughts. "I was a young girl then." She looked quickly over at the viscount with a small smile. "My father had been killed and my mother could not find work. Roland saved our lives by allowing me to help out here at the château. He allowed me the luxury of work during days when most people were grateful for the smallest, most menial task to earn them money for food."

"Enough, *mignonne*, you deserved my help," the viscount said gruffly.

"Perhaps." The viscountess looked at Jean. "But nonetheless, I came here and saw how your father played the Germans and appeared to go along with them while also keeping the confidence of the underground Resistance."

"Papa!"

The viscountess nodded. "Yes, Jean. I saved the book because it was a record your father kept of those people in this community who collaborated with the enemy. It also gave the reasons why, in many cases, people were forced to do this."

"Why?" Eustice asked.

The viscount cleared his throat. "Everyone had their reasons, son. Those were sad days. You have to understand. Some people had relatives being held by the Germans. Others would do anything to keep their families from starving. Almost all of them had reasons. But all of them were dangerous, and I was frightened that if anything happened to me the Resistance would be in trouble without the existence of these records."

"But how did you find out who was involved?" Jean asked.

"Don't you see, Jean? Your father was what they call a double agent!" Eustice's face glowed. "Wow, sir, what a story! Jean, your father is a hero!"

"Hardly a hero," the viscount said bitterly. "You have to understand that the enemy was not stupid. For me to play such games meant that I had to betray some of my own countrymen to avoid suspicion. There is very little to the word 'hero,' son, when you are talking about war."

"But why didn't you want me to know all this?" Jean asked.

"Know all what?" The viscount sounded angry. "That there were times when I did good things and times when I did bad? Is that what you want to know about? Of course it isn't. You want to know the good

things I did. The heroic things as this American calls
them. Well, I wasn't feeling heroic after the war. I
was feeling very tired and ready to forget the whole
ungodly nightmare. And when I fell in love with your
mother, Jean, I wanted it all behind me.''

The viscountess bowed her head.

Jean turned to her. ''But you kept the book, *Maman*. Why?''

''It was the only record.'' The viscountess shook
her head, trying to control the tears that now began
to trickle down her face as she looked lovingly at her
husband. ''You don't tell them, Roland, how it
ended here. Before the end of the war when we knew
the Allies were freeing France after so many years,
they found out you had collaborated with the Resistance. Or suspected you had. So they took your father, Jean, into the carriage house, their dining hall,
where they ate every day, and they shot him, and still
he would not divulge anything.''

''They shot you, Papa?''

''Only in the leg, son. They were nervous about
killing me, they wanted information badly, you see.''
The viscount shrugged. ''But the Allied soldiers
came and found me where the Nazis had left me to
rot.''

''But did one person from this community lift a
finger to help you, Roland?'' the viscountess asked
bitterly. ''No, not one! And so I kept the record. I
kept it to throw in their faces, and I kept it to prove

you the wonderful man you are. I knew you would never tell anyone and I wouldn't have Jean thinking you a collaborator of the enemy. I wouldn't!''

"*Mignonne*, hush. This is all a dream from so long ago.''

The viscount went over and with one hand lifted the chin of his wife so that her face was close to his. With the other he touched the head of his son. "This is what matters to me. And if the enemy chose to let me live so that I could have the last forty years with you, then I am grateful.''

Jean's face shone with pride. "Oh, Papa, I am so glad I found this out.''

"Perhaps, son, it is for the best. But you must not make me a hero. That is not so. I gave much away to save a few here and there.'' He looked at the young people's rapt faces. "Look at your friends, Jean! How lucky you all are that you have never felt war! Here you are, all from different countries, all facing an even larger problem than we were. You must learn from this nightmare. You must try to understand each other. Nothing is worth what we suffered, all of us. And that includes your country, Hans.''

"Yes, sir, I think my country has suffered as well....''

"Where is everybody?'' Angelica came bursting in, followed by Father Thomas and a gendarme.

"What kept you so long, Angelica?'' Eustice asked.

"Book burning." Angelica grinned, pointing to the gendarme. "We found Pierre with the evidence. Before the police could take it away, Pierre set it on fire."

"Why would he do that when he had to go through so much to get it?" Eustice shook his head. "Sometimes I just don't understand things."

The viscount laughed. "My boy, I find that hard to believe."

"But I don't understand why he burned the book."

"Perhaps by destroying it right then and there he confirmed that the record no longer existed in front of his friends." The viscount shook his head. "In a way I think that was wise. Let the dead be dead. This whole incident will be far better to bear if the book and the copy are both destroyed. Jean, where is the copy you made of those records?"

"Here, sir." Hans reached into his pocket and pulled out the duplicate. "I thought it would be useful in case they already destroyed the original."

"Right you were, too, Hans. Good thinking!" Eustice smiled. "Boy, this has been some night. One of the best I've ever had."

The viscountess burst out laughing, got up and went over to give Eustice a tight hug. "You are quite the courageous one, little American."

"I didn't mean it like that, Madame. I'm just glad that Jean found out that both his parents are terrific. And I'm happy that we won't have to worry about being killed," he finished with a grin.

"And we are also pleased to be guests in your home again, Roland," said the countess de Menat with a smiling glance at her husband.

The count nodded. "Yes, you shut off after the war, Roland. Even from your friends."

"See?" Sabine squeezed Eustice's hand. "They are friends again!"

"We have always been friends, Sabine," the viscount said. "It's just that my injury—and perhaps my memories—made me isolate myself."

"So what are we going to do with the copy?" Eustice asked, keeping a tight hold on Sabine's hand.

The viscount took the copy and went over to the fireplace. Turning to Jean he asked, "Son, do you have a match to help me with this?"

"One moment, Papa." Jean ran into the kitchen and returned holding a box of wooden matches.

"And will you help me?" The viscount held out the copy while Jean lit the pages. As the spark caught and the paper began to curl into flames the viscount dropped it into the fireplace and left his hand resting on the shoulder of his son. Everyone watched as the book burned quickly. When the flame died out the viscount said, "I think that this calls for a celebration. Danielle! We need champagne for our guests!" Turning to the room in general, he continued, "You have left one dinner behind. I hope you will share the mysteries of our larder with us to-night."

"That's a mystery I could sink my teeth into!" Eustice said with enthusiasm.

"But Roland, if you do not have enough?" the countess de Menat asked.

The viscount smiled at his wife. "I think we have enough, don't you, Michelle?"

"I'm sure we do," the viscountess answered.

The viscount limped over to the table to take a glass of champagne. When he saw that Danielle had passed it all around, he raised his glass.

"To peace!" he said. "And to the sweet mystery of life!"

"I'll drink to that!" Eustice whispered to Sabine. "Now there's a mystery I can never hope to solve!"

Rachel, standing beside him, blushed as she felt Jean take her hand and squeeze it. "Nor I," she murmured.

QUANTITY	BOOK #	ISBN #	TITLE	AUTHOR	PRICE
☐	161	06161-7	A Chance Hero	Ann Gabhart	$1.95
☐	162	06162-5	Riding High	Marilyn Youngblood	1.95
☐	163	06163-3	Blue Ribbon Summer	Nancy Morgan	1.95
☐	164	06164-1	On the Loose	Rose Bayner	1.95
☐	165	06165-X	Blue Skies and Lollipops	Janice Harrell	1.95
☐	166	06166-8	And Miles to Go	Beverly Sommers	1.95
☐	167	06167-6	Blossom into Love	Norma Jean Lutz	1.95
☐	168	06168-4	Birds of Passage	Miriam Morton	1.95
☐	169	06169-2	Orinoco Adventure	Elaine Harper	1.95
☐	170	06170-6	Video Fever	Kathleen Garvey	1.95
☐	171	06171-4	Write On!	Dorothy Francis	1.95
☐	172	06172-2	The New Man	Carrie Lewis	1.95
☐	173	06173-0	Someone Else	Becky Stuart	1.95
☐	174	06174-9	Adrienne and the Blob	Judith Enderle	1.95
☐	175	06175-7	Blackbird Keep	Candice Ransom	1.95
☐	176	06176-5	Daughter of the Moon	Lynn Carlock	1.95
☐	178	06178-1	A Broken Bow	Martha Humphreys	1.95
☐	181	06181-1	Homecoming	Elaine Harper	1.95
☐	182	06182-X	The Perfect 10	Josephine Wunsch	1.95
☐	183	06183-8	Marigold Beach	Jesse Osburn	1.95
☐	184	06184-6	Here We Go Again	Joyce McGill	1.95

Your Order Total $ _____

☐ (Minimum 2 Book Order)
New York and Arizona residents
add appropriate sales tax $ _____

Postage and Handling   .75

I enclose   _____

Name_____

Address_____

City_____

State/Prov._____ Zip/Postal Code_____

FL-RO2A

WATCH FOR THESE TITLES FROM FIRST LOVE COMING NEXT MONTH

FOLLOW YOUR HEART
Dorothy Francis
Denise gained the courage to make some important decisions with the help of a strange boy who was washed up by the sea.

WALK WITH DANGER
Susan Rubin
When Sharon decided to stalk a dangerous criminal, she found an unexpected ally in cool, streetwise Val DeSantis.

FALLING FOR YOU
Lisa Swazey
Amanda joined the summer theater to get away from her family and an impossible romance. Unfortunately, the scenario turned out to be at odds with her script.

THE JOURNAL OF EMILY ROSE
Jeffie Ross Gordon
Had Jana stumbled on a tragic secret, or was she the victim of her own vivid imagination?

First Love from Silhouette